SALOONS & STARDUST

A COLLECTION

PAMELA JEFFS

Published by Four Ink Press 2019
Copyright © 2019 Pamela Jeffs

Cover design: SelfPubBookCovers.com/FrinaArt
Formatting by Four Ink Press
Language: Australian English

ISBN:
978-0-6481442-3-6 (pbk)
978-0-6481442-4-3 (e-bk)

Visit www.fourinkpress.com

For Maria and Margaret.
Mothers. Friends.
Courageous women.

Reviews

With her poignant and wistful prose Jeffs has the ability to effortlessly immerse you in these dark and wondrous tales. Each story catapults the reader into a different world, dense with history, pain, and hope. A vivid and fascinating collection.

Aiki Flinthart, author of the Kalima Chronicles

Contents

Introduction

Courage

(noun)

The quality of mind or spirit that enables a person to face difficulty, danger, pain, etc. without fear.

***

Sometimes courage is facing down monsters, guns blazing. Sometimes it's about finding the strength to endure. And sometimes it's about having the guts to do what's right, regardless of personal cost.

Saloons and Stardust is a collection of stories that explores this idea, in particular with regard to courageous women.

This body of work is science fiction in nature with fantastical ideas, characters and landscapes, but the theme is one relevant to our own world. The stories highlight the actions and decisions of 'everyday' women. Not world leaders facing down international threats or brain surgeons with people's lives in their hands, but people whose courage is tested and forged by life lessons. This collection is about women facing certain doom and moving forward anyhow; women who will do what they must to save their family; and women who choose to defy danger and fight for a greater good.

They could be your mothers, your sisters or your daughters.

And these stories are to honour them.

Cards and Steel Hearts

It's hard going, this midday flight across the yellow, windswept prairie. My throat is dry and my fingers are seized on my horse's reins. I'm exposed out here, but I can't afford to stop. The Hawk Riders are hunting for me—the ones who killed my parents and my tribe because they wanted what was not theirs to own. I can still feel the warmth of my mother's blood leaking through my fingers, still see the image of my father lying face down in the dirt. I want my revenge, but right now something greater is at stake. I need to get to the Allies, cousins to my mother's people. They will protect me—and the treasure I carry.

Kohana's stride is even beneath me until it is suddenly not. He falters, and next thing I know, I am laid out flat on my back. I get to my feet, brushing dirt and grass from my buckskin dress and leggings. I wince. My palms are stinging, grazed where they caught a thorn bush on the way down. I flick my hands, the pain eases. I walk over to Kohana.

He's expired.

His body lies stretched out as if he is still running. Front legs straight, rear bent, and his nose pointed into the wind. The breeze catches the black and white feathers entwined in his mane. I curse at the luck fate has handed me.

My bone-handled knife slips easily from my belt. I kneel down and dig the point of it into the muscle crease of Kohana's chest. When I push down, his blood wells thickly around the blade. It drips onto the grass, looking more black than red. The knife then slides deeper, and in slicing down, I am rewarded with a metallic *clink*. The blade has found what I am searching for—Kohana's heart. I pull the knife free and push my fist into the wound. My fingers extend and burrow into the warm flesh. I feel the smooth metal orb, and I pull it free.

I turn it over in my hand. Seeing it makes my grief surge again. Here, I hold my parents' legacy: their hopes and dreams for a nation of allied Indian peoples not ruled by white men. It is a weapon, this steel heart. A weapon my father designed for the people even though he was not born of them. He used the technology of his own people, those who live amongst the stars, to build the metal heart. But I can see the stamp of my mother's artistry in the balanced lines of the steel. Always my parents had worked as a team—my mother the artist, my father the inventor. Their combined efforts were a celebration of art and life.

I look for the display of digital numbers I know to be on the underside of the orb. They are there, glimmering green beneath the streaks of Kohana's blood. Four zeros. I, of all people, should have known better. I should never have let his time wind down. If only the attack on my camp had not been so swift, and I not so hard-pressed to escape, I would have remembered to press the small button beneath his chin to reset his heart.

A keening cry from above draws my attention to the skies. Black pinpricks mar the stretch of watercolour blue. Hawk Riders. No time to lose. I reach into the leather satchel slung over my shoulder. Spare arrowheads clink against my firestones. My fingers travel over the prairie turnips and packets of pemmican I grabbed during my hurried escape. They finally fall on the buffalo hide string-tie bag in the bottom. I pull it out.

I place Kohana's heart on the ground and loosen the string. I tip the bag over, and a small wooden box falls out. It is made from a strange white timber, not of this world my mother once told me. The design is simple, low in height with a sliding lid. On top, the image of a star is burnt into the timber. My father's mark, He Who Came from the Stars. I open it and reveal a small stack of thin leather cards, an image painted on the face of each one. Coyote. Wolf. Buffalo. I shuffle through them, searching for one that will help me most now. Finally, I find it. Smaller than the hawks but nimbler and quicker, she is my best chance to outrun them. I pull free the bald eagle named Kimimela.

I wipe my sleeve across the steel heart. Kohana's blood smears away to reveal the card slot pressed into the metal. Next to it are two small buttons. One green, one red. I, myself, have only ever had occasion to press the green one. I press it now, and then flip the card in my hand over and slide it in. Kimimela's painted eagle eye seems to wink at me before disappearing into the orb.

There is a click and a whir. Next to me, Kohana's body begins to fold in upon itself. His legs double back, his head neatly flattens and his barrel chest disappears. Soon he is a leather card with a picture of a horse drawn on the front. I pick him up and put him back into the box.

The steel heart in my hand begins to shudder. The digital numbers on the side begin to flip, faster than my eye can register. They stop at 9999—as many minutes as to last for seven days. Then an alarm sounds, a low, continuous note. I drop the heart and scuttle to one side. A bright light flashes, and Kimimela burgeons into existence.

She is larger than a real eagle, large enough to carry me on her back. She shakes the impossible length of her bronze wings, unfurling them like draping sheets of canvas. Her bright eagle eyes catch mine. 'Wichahpi,' she says, naming me. 'Star Girl. Time to fly.'

I climb up her side and seat myself between her wings. Her back is broader than a mustang's, and I feel the difference in the stretch of my leg muscles. I lock my arms around her glistening, white-feathered neck. She calls out a long, piercing cry, and then we are airborne.

The rush of air is deafening, loud and electric all at the same time. The ground falls away beneath us, expanding to reveal the far-reaching prairie that ripples like a golden sea from horizon to horizon.

In the distance, the serpentine sweep of river marks the border of my people's lands. Beyond it, grey smoke rises gently against the sky—there lie the tribal camps of our cousins.

Not far now.

But, suddenly Kimimela veers right. My legs tighten around her to keep my seat. A dark brown shadow edged with razor claws sweeps by in a gust of air. I see the outline of a man's back sitting upon it. I glance around.

The Hawk Riders. Five of them.

And travelling much faster than anticipated.

Kimimela's cry is a shriek of fury. She banks left as two hawks bear down on her flank. She spins in the air, her claws raking down the side of one. Blood sprays across the blue backdrop of sky, and the hawk crumples. The man on her back cries out before falling to his death.

Another hawk swoops by. This time I hear the laughter of the rider on her back. A whip hangs loose in his hand. His wrist twitches, and the end of it curls around Kimimela's foot. Her wings falter as she is jerked violently sideways. My hands slip from her neck, and I am suddenly dangling precariously by my legs. I grasp the knuckle joint of her wing and pull myself up. She cries out, and I understand her predicament. With me on her back, her fighting prowess is crippled. I do not begrudge her decision as she twists her way out of the whip and then dips out of the sky. This fight will be better fought on the ground.

Her claws clutch up loose grass and clumps of earth as she lands. I slide off her, feet first, reaching back for my tomahawk as I do. Its weight is comforting in my hand. Kimimela turns and curls her body around me, standing guard at my back. Her scent surrounds me, a mixture of warm feathers and sun-heated skin. Then the four remaining Hawk Riders land in a circle around us.

Their hawks are huge, easily twice the size of Kimimela. Their fierce eyes are black pools ringed with gold. They jostle on their clawed feet; their leather and iron harnesses jangle.

The riders dismount. They are white men, dressed in the leather boots, chaps, and wide-brimmed hats typical of the outlaw gunslingers that terrorize the skies. The one with the whip now carries it coiled at his side; the others have guns slung low on their hips. I recognize these men. My gut begins to roil. They are the ones who attacked my camp.

'Well, looky here, Boss,' says the man with the whip. 'It's the lil' Indian girl we been looking for.'

I understand the white men's words; my father taught me well. And I don't like the man's tone. I don't like that he called me little. I am fifteen summers old. Old enough to hunt buffalo with my father, old enough to kill a man. I shift my grip on my tomahawk. Kimimela shuffles behind me. The prairie is silent around us except for the chirruping of grasshoppers.

One of the gunslingers, the tallest one with the dark beard, takes a step closer. His gaze falls on Kimimela. 'That's not a natural beastie you got there, girlie. Definitely got to have a steel heart, I'd say.'

The other men mutter and shift. I can see the greed in their eyes, their eagerness to possess the heart and perhaps to possess me. I will not let that happen.

The leader smiles; his teeth are yellow and broken. 'Hand it over.'

'Come and get it,' I reply.

My words are followed by the sharp crack of the whip. I feel the lick of plaited leather fall across my forearm. It slithers away just as fast, leaving in its place a line of blood. I turn towards the man holding the whip. His leering grin is no more attractive than the leader's. All of a sudden, I am acutely aware of the sun's heat on my forehead, the hot, dry prairie breeze in my nostrils. Of Kimimela, and my mother's cousins too far away to help me now.

I lunge towards the whip man and, before he can blink, my tomahawk has split his skull. It cracks like a melon, the features of his face lost in a sheet of hot blood. Kimimela is attacking the next man, but he is fast. His gun is clear of its holster, but his grip on it is uncertain. The weapon tumbles into the grass. He ducks to retrieve it. I have no time to see what happens next.

The leader grabs me from behind. I let my joints go slack, and I slither free of his grip. I turn and swipe at him with my tomahawk, but he dodges to the side.

I follow and find myself looking down the barrel of his gun.

'Get up,' he growls. 'And lose the tomahawk.'

I do, letting my weapon slide to the ground. I glance about. The fight is over before it has started. Kimimela is captured. Her bright head is held beneath the talons of one of the hawks, pushed hard into the trampled earth. Her wings are spread out awkwardly across the grass, their surface tattered and marred with streaks of blood. She calls out to me, and I feel as if I have failed her.

I look back at the leader. His weathered face is stern. The gun he holds has not moved. 'Get me the heart,' he says.

I nod and tip my chin over to Kimimela. 'I will need to go to her.'

The leader nods and moves to position himself behind me. His gun stays aimed on me, but is now pointed at the back of my skull. 'Walk,' he says. 'And no funny business.'

My heart breaks when I get to Kimimela. I kneel by her side. Her eagle eye swivels up to meet mine. Its brightness captures the light of the sun overhead. The hawk's talons have torn at the flesh on her face and neck. Her lush feathers are coated in her black-red blood. I place my hand on her shoulder, wishing I could somehow warn her of what is about to come.

'Now.' The leader shoves the barrel of his gun hard against my skull.

My head jerks forward, making my teeth clatter. I turn and glare at him. 'My knife.'

He tips his chin up in consent. I reach down and close my fingers over the bone hilt. I lift it. Kimimela's eye follows the line of the blade as it crosses her field of view. Her gaze snaps back to mine. Now, she understands.

I place my free hand on her polished beak. She blinks, and then keens a soft cry. 'Fly free,' I whisper.

Her end is not painless, but it is quick. I draw the blade across her neck. The pupil of her eye widens, her back arches, her claws scrabble at the earth, and then she falls still.

There is a moment of silence, but then I feel the press of the gun barrel again. The leader's voice is harsh. 'The heart,' he says. 'Now.'

I don't bother looking at him. Instead, I pull aside Kimimela's lax wing and plunge my knife into her feathered chest. The blade crunches past her breastbone and into her body cavity. I feel the warm rush of her blood coat my hand. I push deeper. The metallic *clink* follows. I remove the knife and push my fist into the opening. Kimimela's heart is closer to the surface than Kohana's was. I pull it free with a slurping sound.

I lift the gruesome prize, holding it high for the men to see. My fist, arm, and the heart are coated in dark blood. I smell the iron in it and hear the buzzing of the flies already gathering to drink.

The leader reaches around and takes the heart from my hand. His skin is rough against my fingers. He wipes at the blood. The heart emerges, coloured in patches of silver and red. 'We got our prize, boys!' he says.

His grin is filled with triumph.

His attention is not on me.

Stupid man.

I flip the bloodied blade in my hand. Next thing, it is buried in his throat.

His cry is short and sharp, quickly fading to a gurgle as he falls to his knees. He is dead in moments. As his grip weakens, the heart tumbles from one hand, and his gun slips from the other. I scrabble to get the weapon, but a gunshot from one of the other men sends it skipping away from me. Instead, I reach for and succeed in retrieving the heart. I twist on my heel and get to my feet. I stop, looking at the remaining two men. One is wearing a red bandana, the other a faded yellow one. Both have their guns aimed at my heart. Yellow Bandana has his gaze levelled at my breasts.

'That's a mighty silly thing you've gone and did,' says Red Bandana. He is younger than the other man but seems to hold the authority.

'Let me at her. I'll teach her a lesson,' says Yellow Bandana.

A look of disgust crosses Red Bandana's face. I can see he doesn't like the other man. 'Give me the heart, girl,' he says. 'Show me how to use it, and I'll let you live.'

He will let me live? I almost laugh out loud. 'Come closer then,' I say.

Red Bandana moves cautiously. He reminds me of a coyote—sly, wary and clever. In moments, he is standing before me, his gun still held steady. Up close, he is handsome for a gunslinger with his smooth, clean skin and neat, well-tended clothes.

'Show me,' he says.

I turn the heart over in my hand. The green numbers are flipping over. 8199…8198…8197… My thumb traces the line of the card slot and brushes over the green and red buttons.

The red button.

The answer to my problems.

'Put the card in the slot,' I say. 'Press the red button.'

'Card?' asks Red Bandana.

I pull the wooden box out from the satchel still slung across my chest. I open the lid. The Coyote card tops the deck. A good omen, he is the trickster. I pick him up. 'A card like this.'

'So you slot in the card and press the button?'

'Yes. The red one. The green one will destroy the heart.'

The man nods. 'And when you want the heart back, you kill the beastie and cut it out?'

His lack of humanity disgusts me. 'Yes.'

'And where do yon cards come from? How can I get more?'

I am inspired by the Coyote's trickster nature. 'Make them. Leather and paint. Easy to do.' The idea is not so far from the truth, but enough for it to be a lie.

Red Bandana smiles, and with that simple gesture, I understand he does not intend to keep his word. Given the information, I suppose he feels he has no reason to.

He moves quicker than I expect, does not even hesitate as he pulls the trigger. I hear his gun fire, see the smoke bloom out of his gun barrel, and then I feel the searing bullet tear though my chest.

I feel it hit my heart.

I hear the metallic sounding *clink*.

The bullet stops dead.

I look down at my chest. Blood, more black than red, stains the front of my dress. I look back up at Red

Bandana. He looks confused. It's my turn to smile. 'Not all creatures with steel hearts are obvious,' I say.

Then I press the red button.

It is the first time the weapon has ever been used against humans. My father had planned to do it next summer—to go and stand at the centre of the gunslinger's town and use the heart to make the place fold. But his untimely death saw the chance taken from him. Time to even the score. I take a breath and brace myself.

The heart's alarm sounds. I place it on the ground and step back. The sound grows increasingly louder. Stupidly, Red Bandana reaches down and snatches it up.

Then—the alarm stops.

A flash of light, brighter than the sun overhead, illuminates the prairie. My smile widens as I stand in the blaze, protected from what is happening by virtue of the steel heart that beats in my chest—the heart my parents made for me, so they could have a child when nature failed them in that quest.

The light fades. Red Bandana stands frozen. His eyes move wildly, but he has no control over his body. Slowly, he begins to flatten. His arms fold in on himself, his face becomes flat. I can see he wants to scream, but it is too late for that. Behind him, Yellow Bandana falls sideways. He too begins to flatten, arms, legs, and torso losing dimension. Kimimela's body follows, as do the four hawks, all jerking as they try to fight the process.

Soon, I am standing alone on the prairie. Scattered on the grass are nine leather cards, an image painted on each one. One is Kimimela, her eagle eye winking at me. Four hold pictures of hawks, and the other four, images of white men—one holding a coiled whip, another sporting a dark beard. One wears a red bandana, the other a yellow.

I reach down and pick up Kimimela's heart. It is one of only two that exist, the twin being the one in my chest. Both are weapons that can create life as easily as they can take it away. I reach up and press the button beneath my chin. The steel heart in my chest resets. I bend down and collect the cards lying on the grass. The ones of the men will help to light my fire tonight. But the hawks I will keep. Once re-trained, they will prove useful.

My thoughts turn to the Allies—of how I will join them, and together rid the lands of all white men. I will finish what my parents started. I place the cards in the box, holding back the one of Kimimela. I slip it into the steel heart and watch as she burgeons into life.

In Salt and by Starlight

Salt makes them linger, but starlight reveals them. The haunts. The sea is filled with the enraged memories of slaughtered whales, so much so that men can no longer safely sail the oceans. But I am no man. I am a woman and will hunt the dangerous spirits until I can reclaim back the seas for my kind.

I pull back on the tiller of my solar air-skiff. The power gems in the mast flare bright and the wind panels lining the hull open, like scales on a fish, to slow the ship. My vessel lowers itself out of the sky, clouds streaming behind the stern as it reaches for the water. I let the keel kiss the tops of the waves. Sea foam sprays outward, two fans of white against the silver hull.

I can almost smell him—the haunt of the giant male sperm whale. He swims nearby. Having evaded me for the past week, he has proven wilier than most. It seems he can sense when I am close. Because, when the stars are out and I have a chance to capture him, he dives deep to evade my net. It has been a long and tedious chase, but I respect the haunt's tenacity. I wonder if he gave the ancient whalers such trouble when he was alive.

With the touch of a button, the air anchor spools free. I watch it float upward into the starlit sky. The scythe-shaped hook rises, searching for the warmer currents that will catch and hold the craft steady.

I walk to the rail. Its polished steel finish is cold in my grip, but the warm thrum of electricity, harvested by the solar sails during daylight hours, vibrates through the metal. It is encouraging, proof that the skiff is well powered and ready for the fight to come.

The evening air, smelling of iodine and salt, rushes up to meet me as I lean over the rail. I search the ocean. The indigo water ripples in the breeze, the fine chop fracturing the reflections of the stars overhead.

But even with such restless movement, I see him.

The haunt hangs just below the water's surface. His wide back glimmers silver in the starlight, his fins dip and rise gracefully. But even the imperfections rendered by the rippling water cannot hide the history of his death. His hide is marked in shades of black, the places where ancient barbed spears caught in his flesh. This close, I can see gossamer threads of ghostly blood still trailing from those age-old wounds.

Like all of his kind, this slain whale would have died a slow death. For a moment, I wonder if those ancient whalers could ever have imagined the legacy their reckless slaughter would leave for their descendants—the legacy of an ocean frontier ruled by ghosts, with only air and earth left for humankind to rule.

I turn away from the tragedy of the past and focus on the now. I glance up. The haunt net hangs ready from the rigging. The wide metallic loops glint dull grey in the dim light. I detach the net's recharging cable from the socket fitted into the mast. Gripping the lever on the control panel above the socket, I release the net.

The metal chain links creak, shifting slowly at first, as the circular net begins to open. Spars rigged to hold the weight begin to move also, swinging their lean lengths out over the deck into clear water. The patterned shadow of the net paints itself across the deck and my skin, staining them like a tattoo. I wonder if the haunt knows what it means, that fall of shadow with its promise of oblivion.

Soon the net is spread wide by the side of the ship. Its web pattern is intricate, shaped like overlapping stars. But the stars have purpose. Their specific layout conducts the current that disperses the haunt. I have tried simpler patterns in the past, but the weave, if anything less, lets the essence of the creatures bleed through.

I flick another lever. The latches on the spar release, the net powers up, a red glow tripping along the wires. Then it hangs in space, hovering—waiting for me to release it. I glance back at the water. The glow of the haunt is still visible. I let the net fall.

But before it hits the water, the haunt has already moved. His blue glow diminishes as he dives deeper into the water. I bare my teeth. 'Not this time,' I whisper and press the control panel again to release my secret weapon.

Weighted hooks. Welded into the outer ring of the net, they spring open, sending the net spiralling deeper than ever before. I know the moment the hooks catch him. My vessel shears sideways in response, rolling into the wind. Waves crash against the side of the skiff, and I lose my footing on the suddenly tilted deck. I curse as my leg catches the side of the mast and awakens a violent pain in my hip. 'Damn you to hell, haunt,' I snarl. He is stronger than I expected him to be.

I scrabble upright, pushing my leg straight despite the pain. I brace myself against the mast before teetering across the listing deck towards the net controls by the rail. The net's cable, tied to the spars, is pulled taut. The metal of it vibrates, singing with the strain as the haunt lunges deeper again. But this time I am ready. I reach for and catch the release lever. The net cable loosens and the skiff rights itself.

For a moment there is nothing but the sound of the cable whining through the spar eye hooks. Then silence. The haunt has stopped his dive. He seems to be waiting. I wait also. Everything is motionless except for where the ocean breeze catches at the edges of the skiff's solar sails.

Then the sky suddenly seems brighter. And the deck does also; both flooded with a cold, blue light. I look behind me, my heart rising into my mouth. There, outlined against the dark sky is a massive tail glowing bright with starlight. The whale. He has surfaced and he is attacking.

The haunt's tail falls. There is no damage as it passes clean through the stern of the ship. But a moment later, his touch is followed by a concussive blast of unearthly connection. The skiff tumbles to the portside then rights herself again. She is not unscathed. Loose cables and power gems scatter across her deck. I try to duck as a gem flies close to my head. It catches me, clipping my temple and sending a trickle of blood down the side of my face.

The haunt hits again. His broad head suddenly appears through the deck sheeting, passes through and then falls back. Another delay, another connection. The ship keels sideways, too far this time to right herself. I curse. Damn this whale. But I'm not ready to concede defeat. I grip a cable still tied to the mast and clip my breather over my eyes and nose. I feel the ship stutter, rally and then finally settle before sinking into the treacherous waters.

**

The ocean does not welcome humans. I relish the feel of the water closing over my body, the weightlessness and the taste of salt. Blood is still leaking from the wound on my head. It blooms in the water around me, a swirling cloud of red and pink. I am surprised that I can see the blood. I had always imagined the ocean to be dark beneath the waves. But it's not. It is bright with the starlit haunts of a million creatures.

Fish, crabs, and corals—they are luminescent in their watery grave. I look about, sucking in another salt-and-blood-laced breath from my breather. I scan the seafloor, feeling my heart sink. I hadn't realized the extent of the haunt infestation. Five lifetimes would not be enough to reclaim these oceans.

My vision is suddenly obscured by a wide swathe of blue light. It is the sperm whale circling me. His broad side obscures my view before it passes again. I twist in the water, following him. Even as scarred as he is, I hate to admit that he is beautiful in his element. As I watch him glide by, I see his eye fixed on me. There is wisdom in his gaze, an ancient intelligence. I am too stubborn to acknowledge it as real. Haunts are just dangerous memories. Memories that kill men. They are not alive. They do not belong on Earth.

I refuse to regret hunting the already-dead.

But as I watch the ghostly spears in the whale's back waver gently in the current, deep down, I suspect I may be wrong—that perhaps by still existing, they still feel; that perhaps I am no better than my own ancestors, the whale hunters of old.

'No,' I chide myself. 'What I do is for the good of humankind.'

'Has there not been enough death? You have taken our flesh, now you wish to do away with the memory of us also?' The words come from the whale. They are filtered through the water; lyrical and sharp edged like the starlight that shows him to me. I don't want to acknowledge him. It is not possible that he should be speaking to me. He is in the first instance a haunt, and in the second a giant fish.

'You know that I am more.'

I do not wish to believe he is reading my mind. I am hallucinating. I don't answer him but it doesn't seem to matter. The haunt keeps speaking. *'The oceans belong to the dead. Humans lost their claim when they slaughtered and poisoned us to oblivion.'*

I can't help myself. I answer. 'The ocean is too valuable to just leave to you. Humankind will claim it back.'

'You would do better to cherish the memories of how it once was.'

The haunt circles again. As he passes, the ocean and its starlit inhabitants are revealed to me again. For a moment I ask myself what it would be like if I succeeded—how would it be beneath the waves, in an ocean without the haunts? The answer is easy to see. As I look about, I see that these waters are barren. Nothing dwells here except the lingering shades of dead creatures. Without them, it would be dark and silent—nothing but an endless stretch of sand, water and ancient bones.

Nothing without the starlit memories of what once lived here.

'But even if I stop,' I say, 'others will come.'

The whale passes by me again. The current made by his passing buffets me. *'And, like you, they will fail.'*

It's as if his words are a war cry. Suddenly the ocean is blazing bright around me, the light from every haunt rising, brighter and brighter, becoming intense enough to blind. I cover my eyes with my hands. The whale haunt's voice thunders around me. *'I will return your ship. Go to your people and warn them. If they come, I am their doom. For I am Memory, and memory is forever. I will kill them.'*

I feel the weight of both his words and the ocean settle around me. And something more. It is my own haunt net. My blood runs cold as it brushes down my back before slipping away in the current. Around me the haunt lights fade until all that is left is starlight and the whale. His next words are clear as they carry through the water to me.

'And if they do come, I'll not let even their memory remain...'

Gunfire, Gas and Ruin

We are protected in the lee of the old bus shelter. I lean in and grasp Claire's hand. She lies wrapped in my jacket, her breath rattling in and out of her throat. I look at her and see my own future, how my life will end. Six days ago, we were infected; two days after our leaders panicked and reduced the world to bones. It won't be long before she changes into an Affected—and not long before I follow in her footsteps.

Claire's skin has turned metallic blue. The tough, hard-working cleaner in my building is almost gone. She's doing her best to fight the process that's claiming her, to fight the changes Huler's gas is wreaking in her blood. I wish I could help her. I wish I could have helped all the others I was meant to protect but failed.

Claire opens her eyes. Her gaze meets mine. Gold sparks of light dance in her eyes. It signifies the beginning of the end. Soon her eyes will blaze, and then I'll need to kill her or run.

'Anna,' she says. 'This isn't your fault.'

My throat tightens. 'I should have gone into that building, not you.'

Claire coughs. 'You didn't know it was full of gas. I've lived a good life. I have no regrets.'

'Still.'

'The others…need you.' Claire coughs again. Her gaze sharpens. 'And you need to do the right thing. Don't let me hurt anyone.'

My throat is burning. I nod, cursing the events that brought us to this impasse—the arrival of alien ships, the shitload of missiles fired, and the scientist John Huler with his newly developed, but untested, toxic gas.

Pity the aliens weren't hostile.

Claire struggles to sit. Her clawed fingertips scrabble against the concrete. I support her back. The fabric of her shirt is damp with sweat. I watch, silent, as she rests her chin on her chest for a moment. Then she turns to look at me. Her hair hangs in threads around her face, her breathing is rapid. Larger, brighter sparks of gold light swirl in her eyes. 'Deputy Prime Minister,' she says, 'It's been an honour knowing you.'

What's left of her natural brown eyes fades. Between one moment and the next, they turn gold, burning bright like coals. She snarls. Her claws strike and rake down my arm. I feel the sudden hot rush of blood slick across my skin.

I don't remember pulling my gun from its holster, but I remember squeezing the trigger. Next thing, Claire is dead on the footpath.

I gag and vomit. *I am not a murderer,* I tell myself. *I had no choice.*

A hand gently pulls the gun out of my hand. It's Zach, one of the other survivors.

'You did the right thing,' he says.

I turn and vomit again.

***

Eight days ago. Eight days since the Prime Minister of Australia ordered the attack against the alien ships. And when Huler's gas was released and the missiles fell, Australia fell. The aliens, Terrians they call themselves, had only wanted to retrieve the bodies of their comrades. The bodies our military retrieved from the saucer crash in the desert, the bodies the Prime Minister refused to hand over.

'We can defeat them,' he said. 'We'll learn more about them, then sell their technology to the world. Imagine the boost to the economy!'

That conversation seems like years ago. And the Prime Minister is dead. This puts me in charge.

Which doesn't mean much. I gave the aliens what they wanted: the bodies of their people. In turn, they have promised to help us.

When I say us, I don't mean me. I can feel the sting of gas in my blood and, last night, the skin on my inner wrist started to peel and show the tell-tale metallic blue.

I look back. We have left the city and are keeping close to the edge of the river. The small group of people with me are ash streaked, dirty and dishevelled. They're not the cream of humanity—not the scientists, or astronomers or engineers, but they are good people. Worth saving.

Zach Bennington is the most valuable of the group. He's a doctor, young and determined to survive. There is nothing he can do to help me.

And then there are the teenagers. A dark-haired boy and two girls. Brother and sisters by the look of them. They won't or can't talk. But they follow Zach and me; their shell-shocked gazes aimed forever forward, their demeanours haunted and silent.

With the city behind, the ash-lined bitumen road runs parallel to the river. A damaged bridge sits off to the left, spanning the waterway. I lead us towards it. My boots squelch in the mud as we approach. The bridge is sharp edged and broken. Below, debris-strewn water flows sluggishly, heading for the sea.

The Terrians' ship waits on the opposite bank. The vessel is the only bright object in the landscape. Its tall, tapered lines seem ethereal against the backdrop of the smouldering forest behind it. The hull of the machine is glowing with an inner light. Pale blue. And even after all the gunfire levelled at it, the ship shows no damage at all. Against tech like that, we're lucky the aliens weren't hostile.

Pity we humans couldn't say the same for themselves.

Grey fog clings to the ground around the ship. It could be smoke from the burning forest, but this close to the spacecraft there's a better chance it's Huler's gas. Either way, we need to cross the fog to get to the ship.

'We're not going to make it through,' says Zach. The teenagers mill around behind, their echoed sentiment reflected in their agitation.

'You want off this planet, we need to get to that ship.'

'That's gas over there,' says Zach.

His face is warm, human. Nothing like what mine will soon become. 'It could be just smoke from the trees. We have to give it a go. It's die here or die trying, Zach.'

He doesn't like it, but he nods. He looks back at the teenagers. 'C'mon, kids. We're on the downhill run.'

***

There is heat in the ruptured concrete surface of the bridge. I can feel the waves of it rising to touch my face. Or maybe it's just me—the sickness burning me up. I twist my way around the exposed spears of reo bar and jump to clear the broken sections of walkway.

Ahead, the others pick their way across the bridge. Their footsteps are quiet scuffs of sound, their breaths loud and shallow.

Step. Climb. Sidle.

I jump across a small hole in the walkway. The concrete slides from beneath my boot, crumbling first before cascading into the sluggish water below. I jump awkwardly, but land safely. I glance down.

There's not only water below the bridge. There are also dry sections. Small islands formed of rubbish and flotsam that have collected around the pylons. As I stare at it, a sea of lights begins to emerge. Gold. Bright. Beautiful.

There is nothing beautiful left in this world. Only danger. And I know what I am seeing. It's a hundred eyes staring at me. The solid gold, glowing orbs that belong to the Affected.

'RUN!' I scream to the others.

***

Zach and the kids pound their way across the last section of the bridge and on towards the ship. The sound of scuttling bodies rises from beneath me. With the gas ahead and the Affected below, the prospect of death surrounds us.

But the alien ship looms large. I focus on it, a beacon of hope, and I run.

My boots hit the ground with enough force to break more concrete. My breath is hammering in my throat. But it's the blood burning through my veins that worries me, and the sudden, deep urge not to run from the Affected, but to join them in the chase.

My vision doubles and I blink to reset it. Gold sparks dance in front of my eyes. I see Zach ahead. I see the children. I can smell their blood and their fear. Their hands are covering their noses as they run. Gas swirls around their ankles.

I look left. The Affected are crawling up the sides of the bank. They are fast, and they are between the others and me. Their blue skin seems to ripple in the unearthly light cast by the alien ship. I swallow the urge to join the pack. I swallow again. *Just a few more minutes,* I beg whatever god might be listening. I must see the others to safety before I fall.

I clear the bridge and head for the ship. As I enter the field of gas, I suddenly smell smoke. I smile. It's not Huler's gas—just good clean smoke.

I am running amongst the Affected, swept away in the chorus of guttural snarls. I find myself snarling with them and check myself. I push my way through them and, in moments, I am leading the pack. Everything I look at seems so bright, edged in gold.

I am meters ahead of the Affected. My fingernails are starting to grow. They are burning, splitting my fingertips as they sprout into claws. Their lengths scrape my legs as I run. Now I am next to Zach. I subdue the urge to swipe at him, to spill his guts.

We reach the ship. The air is humming, crackling with electricity. I push Zach forward and gather up the kids to follow him. I ignore the look on their faces as they see my claws, my blue wrists, and no doubt the glow in my eyes.

Desperately, I bang on the wall of the alien craft. 'Let them in!'

A sudden spear of light illuminates the forest and the bridge. I suspect my Affected eyesight is making everything look so bright. The ship is opening. A tall, triangular, door is forming in the hull to give entrance. 'Go,' I scream at Zach. 'Get inside.'

He turns to run, but at the last moment I grasp the back of his shirt. I feel him flinch as my claws rake down his back. He turns.

'You know what to do,' I say. 'Don't let me hurt anyone.'

'You can count on me.'

The ship has opened, and I see silhouettes of the Terrians, urgently beckoning the others to board. I sob. Everything looks so bright, it hurts me to keep looking but I do.

Then my friends are aboard. Safe. Welcomed into the arms of salvation.

I hold my eyes open against the brightness. I see the outline of Zach. He is standing in the doorway of the ship. I can't see the details of him, but I would recognize his shape anywhere.

His arm lifts the shape of a gun—my gun—the gun he never gave back after Claire.

I realize he knew all along—that I was infected also.

I close my eyes. I know he will pull the trigger. It's what I asked him to do. Just like Claire asked me. I hear the crack of the bullet; feel the shard of searing lead enter my chest.

As I sway, waiting for my body to fall, I think on how my life began.

And how the others will say it ended.

Saloons and Stardust

I hear the scuff of boots on sun-baked earth and the jangle of spurs against rock. Someone's heading towards the saloon. Another Raider? Or something worse? I crouch deeper into my hiding spot beneath the raised boardwalk. I cradle my belly, feeling my cubs within it move.

Boots thud on the boards over my head. I flinch. Dust falls through the cracks. I hold my breath.

'You should come out from under there.'

It's a woman's voice, accented—hard to place. It's enough to tell me she's not one of *them*. Not a Raider. But anything can hide within the human skin I assume she wears. So, I don't reply. I just hunch lower.

The woman sighs. 'Suit yourself.'

Her footsteps are confident as she crosses to the saloon doors. I hear one swing open. It squeaks loudly, a noise that has saved many a man getting shot in the back without warning.

It won't save me.

It didn't save those who now stand dead in the saloon.

I wait to hear the woman's reaction to the scene inside. I expect an intake of breath or a stumble in her step. There is nothing except the sound of her even footsteps continuing over the threshold.

I move cautiously from my hiding place. Dirt clings to my dress. I slither out between two loose floorboards and get to my feet. I peek in through the dusty window.

The woman is wearing the skin of a human gunslinger. She sits on a stool by the shattered bar. Small of stature, she wears a black-feathered cloak that fails to hide her hunched back. A gun belt hangs loosely at her hip; two silver-barrelled Colts nestled in twin holsters. Even from here, I can feel the heat of the silver bullets she carries. This one is no friend to me.

She holds a bottle of whiskey in one hand, a full shot glass in the other. As she tosses the shot back, a strand of her raven hair falls from beneath her slouch hat. I realize it's not hair at all, but a feather to match her cloak.

The woman is ignoring the chaos around her, as if the statues of the people who inhabit the bar don't exist. I feel a rush of anger. How dare she ignore them? They *do* exist. They are all that's left of my friends.

Anger gets the better of me. It inspires courage. I am ready to face her down.

She pauses as I enter the saloon, her re-filled shot glass held halfway to her lips. 'A real mess you've made here.'

'I didn't mean to hurt them.'

'Maybe.' The woman places the glass and bottle on the bar. She turns. A glimmer of gold light behind her eyes betrays her. She's not a Raider. She's worse than that—a hired Hunter.

'I will not let you take me.'

The woman tilts her chin towards the giant octopus-shaped statue half hanging off the crushed end of the bar. 'I am not as dull-witted as that Raider,' she says. 'You will be taken back.'

Panic. The same I felt last night when the Raider dropped his skin, and I realized what he was. It's the panic that unleashed my power, turning everyone to stone.

'You're too dangerous to be left amongst humans.'

'I'm not.'

Part of me knows she's right. Around us, the saloon is a mess, a mess I made. It's not only the crushed bar with its stone Raider, but all the people—the people I turned to stone.

It's Millie the saloon owner standing behind her bar, the kind woman who found me naked and alone on the prairie. The one who cared for me after I escaped the Raiders.

It's little Billy. The toy gun held in his stone hand. The one pointed at the Raider. He stood trying to protect me in the end. A brave child facing down a monster with the only weapon he had.

I feel a knot of guilt tighten in my chest. 'I didn't mean to hurt them,' I repeat.

'But you did. You need to come with me.'

I won't go back.

I can't go back.

My whole life was spent as Raider slave; my power dimmed by the gold stardust collar fitted to my neck at birth. I was lucky I slipped free of it last time. I'll not be made to wear one again.

My children will not be made to wear one.

I curl my lip in anger. I let my teeth and claws extend. My human skin and clothes fall away. My true form is revealed.

'I won't go back,' I rasp.

The Hunter nods. 'Then I've no choice, Wolf.' She steps off the stool. She shakes out her cloak. The feathers ripple and glisten like black metal. Then the cloak begins to lift. Beneath it, her hunchback flattens out. Two long, black scythes emerge, arching up and over her shoulders.

Wings.

My heart sinks. Not just a Hunter. She's Raider elite, a Winged Seeker.

I snarl and leap for her, but she is already airborne. I am tossed sideways, buffeted by the backlash of her wings. I am up in an instant, claws extended. I rake at her feet, and she twists away, rising so the tips of her wings brush at the ceiling.

I glimpse a flash of silver. Her guns are free of their holsters, one in each fist.

Sharp cracks of sound follow them.

One. Two. Three.

Silver bullets pierce my skin.

I yelp, the searing shots in my chest agony. I fall against the broken bar; the tumbled stone Raider tentacle is at my back. My black blood smears its length.

I rake at my wounds. My breaths are sobs. One bullet falls free. It lies on the floor steaming. Two more to go.

The Seeker lands, her guns held loosely in her hands. She looks almost sympathetic as she watches me tear at my wounds. 'You should have come quietly.'

I cough. Blood sprays across my lower jaw. 'Go to hell.'

I give up tearing at myself. Better dead than a slave. I close my eyes.

I try not to think of my unborn cubs. Nor the freedom I tasted—so sweet, so fleeting. Instead, I try to focus on the long peace of death.

There is no peace in pain.

Pain betrays me. My thoughts turn instead to the black Raider Pits where my kind has been imprisoned since the beginning of time, the place where we Wolves mine the gold stardust which fuels all Raider technology. In this place, I relive again my brother falling from a sheer cliff, my mate dying in a rock fall.

My hand travels to my belly. My children will never know that life.

Soft feathers brush against my cheek. I open my eyes. The Seeker is leaning over me. Her silver cuffs sting as she clamps them shut on my wrists. I watch as she reaches into her pocket and pulls free a large needle filled with gold stardust.

So, she isn't going to let me die.

But I can't let her save me with stardust either. A full dose of the stuff will kill my children.

I struggle against my bonds. My wounds open further, blood sheeting down my chest and arms like a black curtain. The Seeker grasps me around the throat. I feel the needle slip into my foreleg, the cold creep of stardust injected into my veins.

'Not like this,' I beg.

The Seeker doesn't stop.

Her mistake.

I call upon my power. I pull threads of it from my blood and fashion a bolt of lightning. I send the gold torrent of heat and light into the Seeker. Her grip on my throat suddenly slips and her wings flare wide.

My power eats into her, turning her flesh to stone. Her eyes blaze gold, and for an instant, she teeters on her heels. Then her gaze dims, and she falls backwards. Her body shatters against the floor.

Silence follows.

Dust falls.

I am alone again.

I twist my blood-slick wrists, and the cuffs slip free. I throw them across the room. The small portion of stardust the Seeker injected into me feels like ice as it works through my veins. I feel it probe against my wounds. The two bullets in my chest dislodge, falling to the ground. The slow process of healing begins.

So I will live.

And my cubs will live.

I force myself to my feet and resume my human form. Cradling my belly, I walk out of the saloon and head towards the far prairie that beckons.

Others will come. I can't stay here.

Blood and Oil

CAHIRA

Ironhide peals off a piercing cry. I look up. He skirts the undersides of the fractured clouds, the edges of his steel wings dipping and catching the moonlight as he flies. For an instant, he is a dragon etched in silver. Then he wheels away to the north, following the line of the steep-sided valley I am hidden within. His direction is the signal. The alien beacon on the clifftop has awoken. Soon, we will feed.

Metal grinds on metal, the sound rumbling like thunder off the rock faces. I press my fingertips to the back of the boulder that is my hiding place and ease myself up. The cliff face opposite me splits, opening to reveal the interior of an underground flight bunker. I grin. The hunt begins now.

An alien oil hauler, sleek and smooth, exits. Its polished silver hull gleams bright against the darker canvas of the valley. The engine whines, a red glow building at the rear of the vessel—the thrusters warming up. Then the shuttle shoots away, heading for the main highway connecting to far end of the valley.

The highway where Ironhide waits.

It has been a month since our last feed, and we are both ravenous. Ironhide's taste is for the machine oil that powers the extraterrestrial tech, and mine is for blood. Human blood was once the preference, but supply for that ended long ago. Now I make do. Tonight, alien blood will fill my belly.

I run. My steps are fleet, powered by the sharp edge of my hunger. The valley around me is a patchwork of shadow and light, the cool night breeze welcome against my skin. As I leap over rocks and clear creeks, my hair streams away from my face, fluttering like a pale flag in the night.

The running motion sends familiar pains slicing across my torso. They have presented more frequently of late. I ignore them, tell myself it's only the blood hunger gnawing at my belly. But deep down I'm sure it's something more. I've said nothing to Ironhide, but my suspicion is that the alien food source is poisoning me.

I beat the shuttle to the highway. Its thrusters glow beyond the tree line. I stop in the middle of the road. My long, oilskin jacket flutters around my leather-clad thighs and then settles. I look up. Ironhide is nowhere to be seen but he is close. The small, distinctive squeak in his metal ailerons betrays him, the squeak that reveals his own hunger, his lack of oil. My estimation has him riding the air currents behind the cloudbank.

The shuttle appears. It wobbles slightly over the uneven ground as it exits the valley to gain the highway. I raise my chin on its approach, wanting the occupants to observe my face and the shape of my body. For all intents and purposes, I look like a human woman. It will be enough to stop them. And I am right. The lights lining the front of the hull catch me in the circle of their beams and the vehicle slows. For a moment, the only sound is the hum of the thrusters. The mirrored windscreen conceals the creatures within the cockpit. But survival breeds experience. I know what to expect when the hatch opens.

The Nashari. Elegantly built and clothed in fitted black uniforms, the silver-skinned aliens emerge armed from the shuttle's cockpit. Long, thin battle spears are held at the ready, tips glowing white with active energy. Their large, black eyes are wide, their movements cautious as they move to the front of the shuttle. Their carefulness is expected. Seeing a living, breathing human would be a shock. It's been a long time since their extinction.

But perhaps whispers of our hunting sorties precede us. These two aliens smell of fear and both keep a cautious eye on the skies.

Ironhide falls silently from behind the clouds. Only at the last moment do his wings snap open, the sonorous clang of their metal echoing off the road. Then his flight flattens out, a ninety-degree turn, and like a bird of prey, he streaks low towards the shuttle. His jaws open, a maw lined with silver teeth. His breath is the hiss of boiling steam and scalding oil.

The Nashari turn. Ironhide's mouth brightens and flames erupt from his hollow throat. The aliens leap aside, clearing the conflagration by throwing themselves into the brittle bushes lining the road. I jump, higher and faster than any human ever could. I land by the side of the first. My reflection glares back at me from the surface of the creature's dark eyes— my gaunt, pale visage, forehead furrowed and scarlet lips peeled back from my ivory teeth.

'Feed quickly, Cahira!' cries Ironhide.

I need no second invitation.

I strike.

Alien skin is thinner than a human's. My fangs sink in like needles through paper. There is no pleasure in the sensation. The Nashari's blood, blue-black in colour and tasting like bog water, floods my mouth. I clench my jaw against the taste. Denying myself food, however distasteful, is not an option. Immortal or not, if I don't feed, I expire.

Behind me, Ironhide attacks the shuttle. Metal shears as his teeth and claws rip the hull apart searching for the oil tanks. Debris rains down around me. First, half of the cockpit and then parts of the engine, but I ignore them. The blood filling my belly is all that matters. It has been too long between feeds, and I am uncertain when I'll get the chance to drink again. Soon, Ironhide finishes savaging the shuttle. Fragments stop falling. He has found the oil tanks. I hear his sigh of relief and the sound of his metal chin scraping as he leans into the tank and begins to drink also.

***

IRONHIDE

The feel of oil sliding down my throat and coating my gears is akin to ecstasy. For long moments I revel in the spoils of our hunt. Food. Alien oil. Without it my soul, the soul my friend Cahira tied to my new body—this dragon-shaped machine made of alien parts—will fade. And should it pass, the accumulated knowledge of all dragonkind will be lost. For as far as I know, I am the last of the Great Drakes.

I lift my chin from the shuttle's now empty oil tank. Cahira is still feeding by the roadside, her movements urgent as she drains the first Nashari and then moves onto the second. Not for the first time, I am concerned by her state of being. Her figure has grown gaunt in these past months, her bones pressing against her skin. She tries to hide it, but I observe with a saurian's eye—a predator's eye. If she were prey, she would not be worth eating.

Cahira finishes and stands. The aliens' blood has stained her lips, turning them to bruised lines in the moonlight. But her eyes are glowing red with new energy. 'Feeling better?' I ask, noting my voice has lost its rasp.

Cahira nods. 'A little. Did you get enough oil?'

'I'll last another month,' I say.

'Good.' Cahira turns and grips the feet of the first alien. 'I'll dispose of these. You clean up your mess.'

I survey the parts of the broken shuttle lying strewn about. Yes. A mess. But there is no shame. Dragons dismember their prey to consume it. I may no longer be flesh and blood, but why would I change my habits? A dragon's soul, a dragon's way.

The first half of the cockpit creaks and groans as I drag it off the road. Once on the rocks, I breathe on it. My fire melts the thin material to slag in moments. It puddles around the rocks and pools in the gravel. The glow subsides. With my tail, I draw clumps of dried grass across to hide the evidence. Nothing good would come from other Nashari finding the wreckage. Better their comrades just disappear. I turn back for the second piece of the cockpit.

But Cahira is already there, crouched by the side of it. She presses a thin finger to her lips. *Be quiet.* I halt and sniff the air. Metal and old blood. And something else. A faint scent carries on the breeze. Fear.

The cockpit shivers ever so slightly.

And then I understand—a third alien hides inside.

Cahira, a black blur, moves to secure the Nashari. Before I can blink, she snatches the creature from the cockpit and holds it hanging by the neck. Its eyes dart from left to right; long legs kick feebly in the air. With her belly full, Cahira won't feed further this night. So it will be a simpler death for this one. A quick snap of the neck. My gears quicken as Cahira's fingers tighten around its throat. The alien's black eyes widen. Satisfaction coils through my metal. These damned creatures deserve every pain under the sun. They fed upon dragonkind, our flesh a delicacy to them. They fed upon us until only I remained. I'd trade my left wing pistons to see every last one of them suffer.

'Wait!' croaks the Nashari.

I blink. Cahira's fingers loosen slightly. The alien slips through her hand, an inch closer to the ground.

'Please. I can help you.' The alien's voice sounds metallic. A yellow light blinks just above its left ear. A translator.

Cahira glances at me. I know her well enough to guess she doesn't trust the creature. She wants to kill it. Yet I am not so hasty. I step forward. 'What could you possibly help us with?'

The alien looks at Cahira and then back. 'Humans. I can give you humans to feed on.' It looks at Cahira again. 'Your kind prefer them. Correct?'

Cahira snarls, her teeth glittering, white pins. She shakes the alien. 'You lie,' she says. 'There are none of that race left.'

The creature's eyes bulge as Cahira's grip tightens again. Her desire to end its life is fully apparent, but her strength is not what it once was. The arm holding the alien aloft begins to tremble. Frustrated, Cahira growls, squeezes harder but still fails to finish it. I frown.

Cahira's state is worse than I suspected.

'Stop,' I say.

The vampire looks at me. 'Why?'

The Nashari's kicks become more frantic.

'Because you need what it offers.'

'No. I don't.'

'You do. Just like I needed what you offered to me not so long ago.' I wait for her to remember, remember the day she found me half dead in the ruins of a smashed city. That day she tended my wounds. And in the ones that followed, she built a new body for me from the wreckage of a Nashari mothership. Her own blood gave life to the metal and tied my soul to it. I am yet to repay that debt to her.

Cahira's shoulders tense. The muscles in her cheeks work. But reason wins out. She lets the alien fall like a broken doll to the road. The Nashari, lying on its back, inhales and coughs. The light by its ear blinks on. 'Thank you, dragon,' it says. 'You won't regret this.'

But a part of me already does.

***

CAHIRA

Ironhide holds hope, but I dare not. Humans died out long ago. From the shadows, I watched their end— saw them fight the alien invaders, watched them drop nuclear missiles and destroy themselves, millions at a go. Governments were ruthless: *Civilian casualties deemed acceptable in the light of worldwide hostile invasion.*

Humans did half the job of securing their extinction; the Nashari did the rest.

My stomach is aching again. The flush of my recent feed has fled, leaving me feeling nauseous. The small fire crackling in the lee of two rocks offers little comfort. The warmth of it barely reaches my skin, and I find no enjoyment in the dance of the flames. My thoughts turn to the promise of humans. Do they really still exist? Can I risk hoping for salvation?

The Nashari captive, bound hand and foot, sits half leaning against a rock. This close, details of the alien's physique catch my attention. Small things I have never taken the time to notice before. The creature's skin, for instance, and the way it glows faintly in the darkness. And how its thick white hair starts further back on the scalp than a human's would. There is also no discernible gender, or at least none I can try guessing at, and no fingernails. This is interesting. On Earth when animals still existed, even the smallest had claws to defend them.

The translator light blinks awake. 'You are unwell,' states the alien.

I turn back to the fire, annoyed the Nashari caught me looking. 'Shut up,' I snarl.

The alien frowns. 'Would you like to know what is wrong with you?'

'I said SHUT UP!'

Ironhide, resting next to me with eyes half lidded, raises his head. Only his face is illuminated by the firelight, his long sinuous body curling away into shadow. 'What are you called?' he asks.

The Nashari hesitates. 'Norvax.'

Ironhide nods. 'Norvax,' he says as if tasting the word. 'What do you know of my friend's sickness?'

The Nashari's liquid eyes are two dark holes stretching into the infinite. 'I can smell the decay,' it says. 'Her flesh is failing.'

My hand flutters to my stomach.

Ironhide's gaze thins.

The Nashari tilts its head to one side. 'Ending. Dying. Such is the consequence of drinking Nashari blood.'

My breath hitches. Another ripple of pain crosses low against my navel as if to confirm the diagnosis.

'Can it be cured?' asks Ironhide.

Norvax shrugs. 'We have encountered others like her on this planet. All try to survive by feeding on us. Most expire. But one stumbled across our human facility. He entered, fed, and was healed before escaping.' Norvax's gaze finds me. 'Your friend should be no different.'

A puff of smoke trickles out of Ironhide's nostrils. 'You had better be right,' he says. 'For if she dies, so will you.'

***

I leave Ironhide and Norvax slumbering by the embers of the all-but-dead fire. The night stretches out ahead, inviting me to extend my senses and read the world. But other than the sound of the wind, there is silence. No frog song from the creeks, no crickets in the forests, no late-night haunting call of a curlew. It's been years since the invasion, with only the more self-sufficient plant life—conifers, grasses and the like—recovering from the initial decimation. Nothing else remains to give Earth identity. Like myself, she lingers, undead.

And, possibly like her, I miss the old sounds of the night.

Ironhide has awoken. He approaches, surprisingly silent for such a large machine. His words are soft. 'Everything will work out,' he says. 'I won't let you die.'

I shrug. 'So I'm healed. Then what? This new human supply, if it exists, will eventually diminish and I'll be back to drinking tainted blood.'

'We will find alternate options.'

'What options?' I gesture into the darkness. 'I can't eat plants, and nothing else lives out there. Only the Nashari. And when Earth's crude oil is mined out, they will leave. With them will go your food source also. We are both damned.'

'Don't give up, Cahira.'

'But I am so tired of the fight.'

'Then let me wage the war on your behalf.'

The dragon's eyes are two bright embers. Determination hovers in his fiery, mechanical gaze. I press my palm to the moulded metal of his snout and sigh. In the face of such loyalty, what choice do I have? I must try and believe what he says is right.

We will survive.

Somehow.

***

IRONHIDE

We fly. The night sky is my domain, for I am the only winged creature left to ride its currents. My wings dip and rise, the air plucking notes of music from their ends and singing a lullaby to the silent earth below.

From this height, the world looks vast, the horizon ever curving to disappear into the planet's circular infinite. Cahira and Norvax cling to my back. The Nashari stinks of fear. The fact makes my heart-forge flare with delight. It is right my command of the skies and of flight affects the creature so.

The moon's wide eye slips behind a cloud. The valleys and wooded hills below us are shuttered into darkness. But Cahira's eyes are sharp. Her hands grasp the welded knuckles of my wings as she leans in. 'Top of the mountain to the north,' she shouts over the rushing wind. 'Norvax claims the compound is there.'

The mountain's shattered profile makes it look like the stump of a lightning struck tree. I wheel higher. The flexible sheeting connecting my wing's structural skeleton bells out, then we start the long glide towards the plateau.

My claws screech against the rubbly ground. Sparks rise from the dragging length of my tail. Norvax shivers, its fingers wound tightly around one of my spikes. But the sight of solid ground revives the Nashari quickly. It slithers off my back and lands on the ground. I huff out a breath of smoke and stoke my heart-forge to let my eyes flare brighter. To my delight, Norvax scuttles away.

Cahira smiles. 'Ironhide won't hurt you unless you have lied to us.'

Norvax doesn't look convinced.

Cahira turns to the mountain's broken plateau. 'Where to from here?'

The alien dusts the length of its black uniform. No smoothing contains its hair, wild and knotted from our ride amongst the clouds. Norvax gives up. 'You will need this,' it says, pulling a control device out of a concealed uniform pocket.

'Show us,' I say.

Norvax presses a button. The mountaintop shakes. The centre of the plateau splits open to reveal a circular entrance lit from below—a doorway into the heart of the mountain—and a stairway corkscrewing into the depths. A chill runs through my metal. Something is not right about this place. I curl around Cahira protectively. Her hand rests against my neck.

Norvax remains expressionless. Its thin-lipped mouth set into a straight line. 'This is our storage facility. You will meet no resistance inside.'

'Storage?' I ask.

'Yes. Human test subjects,' it replies.

Cahira shifts. 'You keep them stored here,' she says. 'Still alive?'

The alien's black eyes glitter. 'Of course. Their bodies are useless to us dead.'

'Of course,' I mutter, trying not to imagine what the Nashari use their captives for.

Norvax straightens. 'My end of this bargain is concluded. Now release me.'

'Not yet,' says Cahira, stepping clear of me. She flourishes her hand towards the entrance. 'You go first.'

The alien's eyes drop. It presses another button on the control, and a flare of electricity ripples across the opening and then fades. A security barrier. I growl, the sound resonating in the cavity of my throat. 'Deceive us again and no amount of human blood will save you.'

Norvax shrugs. 'You cannot blame me for trying.' Then it walks towards the opening, crosses the threshold and heads down the staircase.

Cahira looks worried. 'Are you sure about this?' she whispers.

'No, but I intend to go in any case,' I reply.

Cahira nods. 'I guess we have nothing to lose.'

'Exactly.'

***

The staircase walls are made of a metal that glows just like Norvax's skin. The pale blue light washes out what little colour there is in Cahira's cheeks, making her look more like a ghost than a vampire. We follow as the alien leads us down into the heart of the mountain, the tangled mess of its bright hair an ugly knot hanging against its thin shoulders.

Humming permeates the stairwell. The resonances of the high-pitched notes vibrate against my delicate ear sensors. 'What is that?' I ask.

Norvax's head twists revealing the line of its chin and the edge of one black eye. 'The stasis generator,' it says. 'We are close.'

The stairway ends at another large circular opening. The humming grows louder. We step through into a vast room dominated by a strange device. It can only be the generator. Forged from a copper-coloured material, the dome-shaped apparatus sits huddled in the centre of the space. A single clear pipe feeds into the top, crude oil, black and viscous, flowing through it like molasses. Fuel to feed the machine.

I glance up. Connected to the generator by glistening threads of electricity are long rows of cylindrical, silver pods. They hang suspended from the honeycomb-panelled ceiling like giant cocoons. Norvax points. 'There are your humans.'

The aliens' treatment of the captives is abhorrent. Whatever their faults, the human species deserves a better end than being held comatose in metal coffins. Cahira steps forward. Her eagerness to feed is revealed as she reaches up to touch the closest pod. 'How do we get it down?' she asks.

Norvax slides open a panel on the underside of the pod. A series of lights blink green. It presses a touchpad and the lights turn amber.

The stasis pod shivers, and then lowers from its hook. The capsule's hull clangs gently against the metal floor. Cahira helps to ease it flat. Norvax leans down and presses another button within the panel. The top hatch of the cocoon slithers back to reveal what is inside.

A raven-haired woman with pale lips. She lies clad in the clothes I assume she wore when she was captured—a red, short sleeve top and blue jeans. Her chest rises and falls in rhythm to the lights now blinking on the pod's control panel. She looks to be asleep.

Cahira's nostrils flare as she scents the blood pumping through the woman's veins. My friend's hands tremble. Her hunter's fangs extend from their sheaths to hang past her bottom lip. Cahira looks at me, her eyes catching the strange alien light and glowing like an animal's. A small smile plays across her mouth.

Then she lunges, latches onto the woman's neck and begins to drink.

***

CAHIRA

Something goes wrong the moment the blood touches my tongue. Instead of the rich, creamy texture I remember, the fluid hisses and spits as it mixes with my saliva. I pull away from the human. Two trails of red stream down her neck, the colour seeping into the collar of her shirt. My throat is burning. Really burning. I clutch it with both hands.

Ironhide growls at Norvax. 'What is happening to her?'

The Nashari regards me, gaze imperious. 'I did tell you they were test subjects.'

My stomach heaves. New welts of pain, fiery and furious, lasso across my hips and up my spine. I draw a ragged breath and reach for the edge of the pod. I miss and slither to the ground, racked by a coughing fit.

Ironhide lumbers forward, his tail screeching across the metal floor. His wings are two sails held at half-mast, his bared teeth gleam. 'What does that matter, Norvax?'

The alien smiles. 'These are Human/Nashari hybrids. Created exclusively for the toxicity of their blood to vampires.' Norvax points at me. 'Her kind have been a problem for our operations, worldwide. These modified humans have proven useful in exterminating them.' It smiles wider. 'Your friend was certainly sick before, but now she will die!'

Ironhide roars. The noise sends the still hanging stasis pods to swinging. Norvax looks up. Momentarily distracted, it doesn't notice the dragon's maw open or the ball of raging, oil-fed fire boiling in the back of his throat.

But it does scream when Ironhide's flaming breath engulfs it.

Norvax incinerates in seconds. When the flames die, all that remains is ash and the oily smell of scorched alien flesh.

Ironhide leans over me. His metal eyes are wide, the gold flames dancing in them filled with regret. I rest my forehead against his front leg. 'It isn't your fault.'

'I made you come here.'

'It's all right.'

A growl rumbles deep in Ironhide's chest—his heart-forge raging in response to his frustration. 'But I owe you a life debt,' he says. 'If only I had the parts to build a body as you did for me.' He shakes his broad head. 'I would trade places if I could.'

I laugh and it makes me cough again. Another slice of pain whips across my belly. I grit my teeth. 'Vampires are damned, remember; we don't have souls.' I suck in a sharp breath. 'There would be nothing of me to put into the metal. Only my blood.'

The dragon pulls away from me. His eyes are spinning points of light. I wonder if they seem brighter because my vision is dimming. 'Then if that is all that remains,' he says, 'gift it to me. Pour your blood into my metal. And I will forever honour your memory.'

And because he is my friend, I do as he asks.

The scar on my palm is a knotted cord of flesh against my lips. It's the place where I bit myself to feed and quicken the metal body I built to save Ironhide's soul. My blood tastes bitter, tainted by poison flowing through it. Ironhide lowers his head to me. I lock my bloodied palm to his cheek. His bell-tone sob of grief is the last sound I hear.

***

IRONHIDE

The Nashari departed Earth two days ago. Exactly two years after they killed Cahira. But their exodus does not concern me. The blood my vampire friend gifted me, freed me also. With it flowing through my mechanical veins, I no longer need the aliens' oil to feed. The nature of my soul has been re-forged. Now it is self-renewing and independent of the fuel once needed to sustain me.

I am the newest of Earth's races—a hybrid born of three.

Alien, Vampire and Dragon.

My wing beats fall steady. Below me, the landscape passes in a wash of blurred colours. Green. Red. Blue. The lack of definition speaks to me, recalls to me the Earth and the grief carried in her silence. To that I can relate. I roar—a promise carried in the sound. 'Mother Earth,' I say. 'Here I am! I pledge to cleanse your lands and raze the Nashari compounds to the ground. Your damaged children, the humans, shall be returned as ash to your soil. Then I shall scour the world and find Cahira's kin. With alien technology, my dragon's wisdom and vampire's strength, I will devise a way to make them like me—a way to give them new bodies by binding their consciousness to alien metal and so freeing them from their blood hunger. Then together we will forge others, other mechanical creatures to fill your silent lands, seas and skies.

And when all is done, we will be one race.

We shall be named Cahiraans.'

Revelations

I love the smell of raw steel and the feel of metal shavings crunching beneath my feet. It's an unusual trade for a woman, being a blacksmith, but my hands are broad and built to wield hammers and pull files. They are hard hands, but clever. Their skill enabled me to buy my freedom and a smithy of my own after a full sixteen years of slavery.

I run my file down the almost-smooth cheek of the figurehead I've been commissioned to remake. She will replace the one damaged on *Althea's Run*, the space galleon captained by the Governor's pirate-hunter, Captain Bayard. The work is cathartic, the pulling of Althea's beautiful face from the metal. I have made her eyes wide-set and framed by a tumble of curls. She is exactly what I imagine a daughter of mine to look like.

If only I could have children.

I curl my fist around the file. My knuckles pale to white. There will never be daughters for me. My legacy is destined to be my art and a heart full of parental hate.

The doorbell over the workshop entry sounds out. The small chiming sound is delicate; not so delicate is the mountain of flesh that follows it.

A man, built like a cliff, bursts through the door. His steel-grey hair and sun-weathered skin mark him as a sailor type. A green bottle hangs from his hand. He runs through the workshop but trips, his boot catching the edge of the pile of lumber stacked by the forge. He falls, lands face down on the ash-strewn floor, and is still.

My stool scrapes the flagstones as I push it back. Metal shavings tumble off my leather apron, a glittering curtain swept away by the breeze blowing in from the open door. I stride over to the man. With my boot I roll him over.

A brand glares at me from his upturned wrist. Irrefutable proof this man is a criminal. And not only that. He's a thrice-damned pirate like my parents, Jon and Liza Lester were. 'Did you abandon your child on the streets of New Providence as well?' I mutter. 'Get up and get out.'

The man seems dazed. His mouth moves but the words are mumbled. Perhaps the fall has concussed him.

His hand twitches. The green glass bottle rattles against the flagstones. I kneel down to pry it free. The man flinches, his grip tightens.

His eyes blink open. Sea green. A colour that almost matches my own. His gaze locks onto mine. A flash of recognition, then he pushes the bottle into my hand. 'Please,' he says, his words suddenly clear. 'Take it. Hide it,'

And I do. The vessel is concealed in my apron pocket just as three mechanical guardsmen burst through the door.

Their copper limbs gleam in the light filtering in through the doorway. The governor's brand imprinted into each of their chest plates glows with the light of the power gems fitted behind them. The guards' expressionless faces scan the room. They see the man.

'There,' states one, his voice a series of mechanical clicks.

'Take him,' says the next, sounding identical to the first.

The pirate scrabbles to his feet and swings at the lead android. He misses. The guards, their strength inhuman, grapple with the man and throw him to the ground again. He lands with a heavy thud. The guards show no compassion as they clasp iron cuffs to his wrists and ankles. I almost feel sorry for the pirate. Seeing him bound like that—it reminds me of an aged draft horse being led to the slaughterhouse.

The man struggles. I respect his determination. But the guardsmen give him no quarter. They twist the pirate's arms backwards. He cries out before he is again subdued.

The man's gaze, still defiant, meets mine. 'I'm sorry, Pandora.'

A shiver crawls down my spine. I have no idea how this man knows my name. Nothing about him is familiar to me. I stand silent, uncertain, as the guards drag him out the door and away down Industry Street towards the jail.

The third guardsman, Sheriff Clockman, remains in the workshop. His mechanical eyes swivel strangely as he takes in the lay of my smithy. The quiet hum of his motors fills the silence. Then he speaks, 'The pirate knows you?'

'So it would seem,' I reply. 'But I assure you, I've never seen him before.'

'Did the pirate say anything else to you?' asks Clockman.

It was Clockman's cold hand that dragged me to the Slave Guild all those years ago, Clockman's precise hand that sterilized me so I could never have children. For that reason alone, I lie to him. 'Nothing.'

'Did he give you anything?'

The bottle suddenly feels heavy in my apron. 'No.'

The hypnotic spin of the Sheriff's irises slows.

He may be suspicious but he can't prove anything. I ask a question of my own. 'Who was that man?'

Clockman's gaze flickers across to the broken doorway and then back to me. He seems to hesitate, his metal limbs rigid as he considers me. The moment passes. 'Bold Jon Lester,' he says. 'He and his pirate crew were apprehended attempting to steal the *Althea's Run.*'

Clockman's casual mention of my real father's name unnerves me. My vision wavers. I swallow, fighting to keep my expression neutral. The skill hard learned as a slave serves me well now. 'Jon Lester?'

'Yes,' replies Clockman, his voice cold. 'And he is scheduled to be terminated at sunset.'

Terminated.

He means hung by the neck until dead.

But I have no interest in letting Jon Lester die. He is the only one who can give me an answer, an answer to the question I've spent a lifetime asking.

Why was I abandoned?

Finished with his questions, Clockman bows and turns to leave. As he does, my mind is already working on a plan to free my father.

***

It'll need to be sunset before I go for Bold Jon. In the meantime, I inspect the bottle. The glass is worn, almost opaque with its motley collection of scratches. The neck is corked and sealed with red wax. I pull a thin, flexible file from my toolbox and guide it in along the edge of the seal. The sharpened tip slides easily through the stopper. Wax crackles and falls to scatter on my scarred timber worktable.

I tip the bottle over. A small roll of paper slithers free. I ease it open and lean in towards the lamplight. The document is fragile, the paper worn to translucence. Across the surface crawls a tangle of faint brown lines outlining a jagged coast, an unnamed reef, a lagoon protected by cliffs. But it is the bold, blood-coloured 'X' in the top left hand corner of the map that has my attention.

Treasure.

Thoughts crowd my mind.

Is this why Bold Jon and his crew were going for a ship?

What treasure would a man like him hunt?

Gold? Power gems?

A more personal question comes to mind.

Did he come to New Providence looking for me, or was it by chance he fell into my workshop?

I glance out the window. The sun huddles low over the industrial quarter buildings. It's almost time.

Time to get answers.

Time to save Jon Lester.

With trembling fingers, I re-roll the map and carefully slip it into my sleeve. Anxiety sours my stomach. I am unable to decide if I relish or fear the encounter to come.

***

The streets to the gallows are filled with food vendors setting up for the evening. The greasy, thick scents of fried fish and grilled flatbread carry towards me on the light wind blowing in from the docks. Any other time I would be tempted to stop and eat, tempted to socialize. But this evening my focus is elsewhere.

There is already a raucous crowd gathered in the hanging ring. Old matrons with salt-stiff skirts, burly sailors, their palms knotted with calluses, and loud-mouthed drunkards. All stand about, shouting, muttering or cussing, anticipation running high as they await the executioner.

The gallows stand central to the courtyard. The wooden structure towers above the people, the noose sways gently in the breeze. Such a primitive way to kill in a world filled with technology, but it's a way that appeals to the people—and a way to control them. The guards encourage the spectacle as a warning for humans thinking of causing trouble.

I slide further down the street, hugging the line of buildings. At the far end are the jail cells. Behind the bars, the twelve men that fill them can be seen. Jon Lester's crew, no doubt. They are a motley bunch, both young and old. Many sport injuries, black eyes, and arms nursed in makeshift slings. It looks like they gave the guardsmen a good fight. What kind of man is Jon Lester that so many would follow him to their deaths?

A good man?

A decent one?

No.

My stomach knots on the bitter taste of old hate. Bold Jon is the man that left me as a seven-year-old child to fend for myself on wicked streets.

Skirting the outer edges of the crowd, I make my way towards the jail. I pass the baker's son, his face red with his hollering. The fishmonger's wife—'Kill them bastard pirates,' she screams, a skillet brandished in her small hand.

When did this town become so full of hate?

The jail building is relatively new. The painted, timber plank walls stand stout, but while clean last summer, they are now weathered and stained dark with gull droppings. I work my way around to the back of the building, cursing as my boots slosh in a puddle of mud that reeks of rotting fish guts and cat piss. I continue past the first cell and on towards the next—the cell with the weak point.

It's a weak point learnt about last New Years Eve. The night when warm ale sloshed over my knuckles as the builder's daughter, drunker than was wise, had toasted me, declared me her friend, and then shared her father's secret.

I feel around the bottom edge of the third plank up from the ground. A solid pull and the timber comes away. The girl was right…her father had saved gold by using silicone to fix the logs at the back of the building, not concealed screws like at the front. I shake my head. Everyone, even the tradesmen, is a pirate in this town.

I hear the click of a key in a lock and the clang of steel. A cell door opens out the front. Time is running out. I reach in and pull again. Another plank tumbles free. I shuffle back, letting it fall to the ground. A small, dirty face peers out of the hole in the wall.

It's a boy, no more than ten, with startling blue eyes. 'Thanks for the bust out, Ma'am!'

He is small enough to slither out of the hole in the wall. Once free, his gap-toothed grin is full of mischief. He winks at me. 'Ponch is the name.' His smile widens. 'Let's get the others.'

With the first plank free, the others are easy to lever away. Men, one by one, crawl free. But none of them are Bold Jon. Out the front, there is the sudden snap of falling timber, a short, sharp cry and the creak of a rope pulled taut. A sudden surge of adrenaline rushes through me. Was it Jon? Am I too late?

But then I hear the mutters from the men behind me, 'Fare thee well, Tom.'

Not Jon but another. Then the men are moving again. No chance to pause for grief.

'Cap'n is in the next cell,' whispers Ponch, his eyes wide with fear.

I smile to reassure him, 'Then it's one more cell and we're out of here.'

With the help of three men, five more planks are pried free to give Bold Jon his freedom. He rolls out of the opening with a grunt and a groan, landing on all fours. 'Thank ye lads,' he whispers. 'Although hanging might have been better than this headache old Clockman gave me.'

I hang back as his men gather around, helping him to his feet. My hate for the man boils in my chest. How dare Bold Jon sound so reasonable. How dare his men love him so.

But there is no time for conversation. A scuff of boots sounds out from around the corner of the jail. I glance back. It's Clockman with six guardsmen. A blaster held in his cold, rigid fist.

His eyes fall on me. Their irises stop circling for a moment then resume, spinning faster. 'Recognized your father then, did you?'

How did he know?

The Sheriff's head tilts.

He fires.

The sudden crack of laser-fire is followed by the sickening stench of burnt flesh. The man next to me slumps sideways, his linen shirt stained with blood.

A pause—a heartbeat long.

Then chaos erupts.

As the condemned men flee, a small hand slips into mine. Ponch. Bold Jon stands next to him. 'Time to leg it, lass,' he says to me.

***

We run through the back streets. My boots pound the mouldy cobblestones; the stink of human excrement surrounds me. My breath comes sharp and heavy, my mind races. How did Clockman know I would help the pirates? If caught, no doubt I'll swing with them.

The smell of salt is suddenly on the air. A cool breeze fans my face. We round the corner of a warehouse and are met with the glittering lights of the docks.

Ships of all sizes rock quietly against their mooring ropes. The space freighters, galleons and low, sleek zoomers hover over the water, their solar sails fanning like sea eagle wings against the night. The forged metal figureheads appear almost alive in the glow of the power gems that line the hulls beneath them. On any other night, it would have seemed magical.

But tonight it's different.

Tonight I am led by the pirate Bold Jon.

'This way,' he whispers, leading me towards the farthest pontoon.

Ponch bounces at my side, all signs of fear replaced with wild glee. He grins wide. 'Just wait, you're gonna love her!'

'Love what?' I whisper.

'You'll see.'

Bold Jon is silent as he weaves from shadow to shadow. He moves with confidence. He shows no sign of fear. Despite myself, I begin to see him not as a devil, but as a man more capable than most.

A dark shadow looms ahead. The outline of a ship materializes, sleek and elegant. No figurehead graces her bow. No lights illuminate her solar sails. She rests in complete darkness.

Ponch squeezes my hand. '*Althea's Run*,' he whispers. 'Was I right? Do you love her?'

The lines of the vessel solidify as we move closer. Yes, Ponch is right. Captain Bayard's ship is a work of art. Her smooth, metal lines are a testament to her designer. Her polished hull hovers just above the waves, like a dancer floating in air. Ornate rails line the slightly scooped edges of her bow. The faceted power gems fitted to the hull reflect the dock lights like a thousand eyes. Even without her figurehead, the one still sitting back in my shop, *Althea's Run* is stunning.

Bold Jon leads us out of the shadows and towards the ship's gangplank. I am surprised at the lack of sentries but do not question it as I am led aboard. I stumble over a partly coiled power lead that lies on the deck but check myself.

My father stops and turns to me. His rugged face is lined in the orange light from the full moon that has just cracked the horizon. The touch of his large-palmed hand against my cheek is soft. His eyes glitter. A part of me wants to pull away but another part of me wants my father to embrace me.

Bold Jon's voice is a whisper. 'I'm sorry, Pandora,' he says. 'Ye were in my thoughts always.'

The question that has burned in me for so long flows out like molten steel. 'Why did you leave me?'

My father looks away to the docks. They are still empty. He looks back. 'Clockman. He accused yer mother of stealing power gems in the market. I defended her, and in doin' so he arrested us both for piracy. Captain Bayard took us away.' His jaw clenches and releases. 'And then left us on an outer rim island wit' no way to return. A freighter found us only last year.' He runs the back of his hand under his nose. His pirate brand is bared briefly with the movement. 'I've bin looking for yer ever since.'

There is sincerity in his tone. And despite the years of hatred, I find myself daring to believe him. Daring to forgive him.

Damn him.

'Where is my mother?' I ask.

Bold Jon lowers his hand. 'Do ye have the map?'

The map? I reach into my sleeve and pull it out.

'Good lass. Now you'll need to take it and sail for the island. Yer mother is waiting for ye at the spot marked "X".'

'X?'

'Aye, she's buried there.'

My breath hitches as the memory of the blonde haired, blue-eyed woman I once called mother fills my mind. 'She's dead?'

Bold Jon looks down at the deck. His fingers worry the edge of his tattered shirt. 'She died of a broken heart, love. Never got over losing ye.'

Lost in my thoughts, I barely register the shadows of the men that begin to crawl up the gangplank. Bold Jon's crew. They have found their way to the ship.

It's the sound of clanking footsteps that draws my attention back to the present. I glance over the rail. Pounding their way down the length of the dock is a contingent of guardsmen, their blasters drawn. At their head races Clockman.

Bold Jon's large fingers pull my chin around so that I face him once more. His eyes are filled with fierce fire. 'Yer mother was my treasure. As she lay dying, I promised her I would find ye and bring ye to her grave.' He points to the ship's wheel. 'Use the map. Take my men and this ship. Go to her!'

All the anger and the pain I have held against him for years bleeds away. All I can do is nod as he pulls me into a rough embrace. I breathe in the salty scent of him as the heat of his tears touches my neck. Then he steps away, his hands still resting on my shoulders.

'And one last thing,' he says. 'Look after yer brother. He's a good lad.'

Brother?

Bold Jon drops his hands and kneels down before Ponch. He ruffles the boy's hair. 'It's time, Boy'o,' he whispers. 'I gotta go. Now be sure an' help your sister.'

Then Bold Jon is on his feet. As quick as a hammer strike, he is gone. His boots thud on the gangplank and his mighty roar echoes out as he barrels down the dock towards Clockman.

About to run to his aid, I feel a tug on my sleeve.

It's Ponch. My brother. 'Don't break his promise to Mama,' he pleads.

I turn my gaze back the docks. My father, surrounded by guards, is outlined in lamplight. He fights fiercely, not for his life, but for his children and the promise he made to my dying mother. In that moment, I know I'll do as he asks. I'll become what I despise. A pirate. A criminal. And all because I see now that Bold Jon is a good man. A man worth honouring.

I look around at the waiting crew. They all stand uneasy, one eye on the docks, awaiting my order.

No need to delay them longer. 'Heave the ropes, lads,' I say. 'Set course for Jon's island.'

The crew move quietly but quickly. Mooring ropes are slipped from ties, and beneath my feet the ship's engines whir to life.

Then *Althea's Run* floats quietly into the night sky. I stand at the ship's rail, holding my brother's hand. The solar sails above us creak as they catch the wind and we are pulled away. Beneath us, as the docks shrink, I watch Bold Jon Lester.

And I keep watching until he drops.

My broad hand clenches. The map still in it gives, the paper creasing to fit my palm. 'Fare thee well,' I whisper, my voice cracking as the fallen figure of my father diminishes into the distance.

Chimeras at High Noon

I survey the racing herd. The mech-horses stream across the prairie, their metal hides glistening in the noonday sun. My eye falls on the copper animal leading them. It's not Cerberus—not the hematite coloured stallion I lost in my last battle against the desert dwellers. He isn't with this herd. He's close though; so close I can smell him.

'Any of these beasties catching yer fancy?' The Stockman, the only human trader in these parts, leans against the weathered timber rails that make up the stockyards. His reputation has him being all about gold, but the stink of Bora brandy on his breath suggests otherwise. My nose wrinkles in distaste. Bora brandy. The taste of it stays in your system. I know from experience. The gunslinger whose blood I drank last night was intoxicated with it.

'This herd's in poor condition,' I say. 'I was assured you had good stock.'

The Stockman sniffs. He steals a glance at me, and I suspect he knows what I am. 'These mechs are top quality. Nuthin less than second-age war-chimera blood running in their pipes. Tough brutes. And a few dents ain't affectin' the way they run.'

I trace the trigger of the black mech-blaster hanging from my belt. Hydraea. The first-age chimera whose blood powers the weapon isn't impressed. 'He lies,' she whispers. 'These are fifth-age at best.'

I look up. The Stockman breathes out a rancid breath in my direction—not only Bora brandy, but rotting teeth as well. 'These mechs will not serve my purpose,' I say. 'Have you any others?' I press a finger to the money pouch hanging from my belt. The soft, pale leather gives under my touch. 'My gold is good for the right mechanical.'

The promise of coin earns me The Stockman's confidence. 'Well lass, there's one more. A stallion. But he's a wild one. He killed a feller just last week, and that poor blighter weren't the first. The cowpokes that brought 'im in reckon they found 'im in a desert dweller camp. Killed all fifty of the tribe, they say. The mech is set for dismantlin', but for the right price I coul' mebbe speak to the Yard Holder and get 'im off the list.'

He is talking of Cerberus, I am sure of it. So they plan to dismember him? Well, they could try I suppose.

***

The mech-horse *is* Cerberus. They have him corralled away in an iron cage behind the saloon. I refrain from smiling when I see him. No need to give a reason to pay more gold than necessary.

My stallion has lost none of his fire. Cerberus snorts and rears at the sight of The Stockman. The man stops well back from the cage. A moment and the dust settles. 'That be it,' he says. 'But I don't think he's what yer want. He be havin' some wicked malfunction, this one.'

But there is no malfunction. Cerberus is exactly how he is meant to be, exactly how he has always been—wild and savage.

I drink in the details of him. The length of his silver metal mane as it flares against his dark flank and the way his eyes glow red. His shell has a few more scratches than it did before we were separated. And there is a dent next to his nose. But the damage is not bad.

'He's perfect,' I say.

'Perfect?' mutters The Stockman. 'Sounds like you're as crazy as 'im.'

You have no idea.

The Stockman introduces me to the Yard Holder. The overworked android with its dented chest-plate looks me up and down. Scanning me. I stand motionless and let it finish. No official records of my vampiric status exist this far past civilization. The android finishes. 'Fifteen pieces of gold,' it states in its monotone, metallic voice. 'And if I see this mechanical again, I'll dismantle it myself.'

'Of course,' I say, relieving my purse of coin. I am handed a charge key. The android and The Stockman take their leave.

I approach the cage. Cerberus nibbles the bars, his metal lips clanking gently against them. 'What took you so long, Aguna?' he asks.

It's good to hear his voice. 'I had to walk all the way here.'

'Why did you not transfer Hydraea to a new steed?'

'Because,' replies the chimera occupying the blaster, 'I refuse to lower myself to your standard.'

Cerberus growls but holds his words. My two chimeras have an uneasy alliance; one better held if mouths are kept closed.

The charge key slots easily into the reader by the door. A series of whirs and the cage door clicks ajar. Cerberus's eyes brighten then fade back to embers. 'Let us leave swiftly. I long for the burning sands,' he says.

The streets are empty as we make our way out of town. Dust follows in Cerberus's footsteps, billowing up and clinging to his hooves. The midday sun rides overhead. Too bright and too hot. Not enough to burn me, but enough to sting. I pull the cuffs of my sleeves down over the backs of my hands.

We pass by weathered buildings, clusters of dried grass huddled at their foundations. The plants' brittle heads toss gently in the noon breeze and I find that, even dead, there is something beautiful about them. Maybe the way they have lived and died in their time. Not like myself, rendered undead before my twentieth year and exiled to the desert before I ever had a chance to really live.

The red sand dunes ripple in the hazy distance. A lonely, unforgiving stretch of heat and light. As I look across it, I have a sudden desire to linger longer here in town. To be around real people. Cerberus senses my thoughts. 'We cannot stay,' he says. 'The Sheriff will come.'

'Let him come,' I reply, feeling reckless.

'Not that one,' says Cerberus. 'He's dangerous. He belongs to the Star God.'

Fear curls around my heart. I tighten my hands on the reins. Technology long ago replaced the ancient religions. But the Star God—that one was sentient. It refused to fade away. And more so, it harbours no love for my kind. 'Let's go,' I say. But before we take a step, a voice calls out from the saloon steps.

'Halt, stranger.'

Too late.

I swivel in the saddle. The sheriff. He's standing in the middle of the road, a calm, easy smile on his perfect lips. 'We are leaving,' I say.

The sheriff smiles wider. He tilts his chin. The sun catches in his eye, an unnatural green glint revealed in its depths. It's the only imperfection in his otherwise pristine illusion.

'No,' he says. 'You are here for redemption.'

'I came for my horse. Not trouble,' I say.

'And yet trouble has found you. Your kind does not belong amongst the living.'

Hydraea is indignant. She twitches in her holster. I frown, taking the measure of the creature staring me down.

He looks almost human in this light. But the small things give him away. The inhuman glow in his eyes and the fine scaling on his brow. And there is the way his clothes seem impervious to the dust. He is definitely one of the Star God's children—utterly perfect in a way the rest of us can never be.

Well, perfect or not. My hellish soul isn't his for the saving.

'Get off the horse,' says the sheriff. 'Come inside.'

'You really think I'm going to make it that easy, Sheriff?'

'I pray so.'

'I've never found praying to be of much use.'

'Well, let us finish it then.'

On cue, Hydraea leaps into my hand. But the Star God minion is just as fast. His mech-blaster, shining silver, is aimed before I can blink. I smell the chimera that powers the weapon, ancient and full of wisdom. One of the Originals. Powerful.

Powerful enough to kill another mechanical.

Hydraea must sense her too. She shivers in my hand but remains resolute.

Cerberus doesn't move.

Long moments pass. The townsfolk watch us silently from the saloon's veranda.

So it has come to this: Chimeras duelling at high noon.

'It doesn't have to be like this,' says the sheriff, his words all honey and piety. 'I can save you.'

'You're not interested in helping me. You want me dead.'

'Dead, yes. But your soul can be saved. As will those of the innocents you would feed upon.'

'I'll not lay down my pistol to the likes of you.'

The sheriff's mouth turns down. Sadness feigned. 'You feed on the living. There is blood on your hands.'

'Blood is life,' I reply.

I squeeze the trigger. Hydraea's essence exits the barrel. As a ball of green light, she roars, emulating the fully-grown blood-chimera she once was. Her aim is true as she streaks towards the sheriff.

The Sheriff's own chimera soul whines out in return. The Original, also made of light, is so bright she burns. Blinded. I cover my eyes but hear Cerberus stamp his hooves. Then his shadow falls across me, and my vision is restored. But his defence demands sacrifice. And the Original claims it. With a squeal of distressed metal, she collides with him broadside and enters his body. Her pure soul invades his pipes. Her essence skews the programming of the finely tuned nanobites within his blood that maintain the tie of his soul-life to his metal. Then The Original exits him.

Silence.

For a moment I sit reeling. Cerberus stands swaying. A drop of blood falls from his nose and splatters onto the dusty street. The single drop then becomes a torrent streaming from his nostrils.

My heart sinks into my stomach.

Cerberus's dark skin writhes as the molecules within shift and rearrange. His metal mottles, its colour leeching away, turning the hematite to pale silver.

'No!' I cry, dropping my gun and reaching up to grasp his neck; reaching to try and stop the bleed of colour. 'Cerberus,' I whisper, already knowing there is nothing I can do.

My mech-horse is gasping. My palms are covered with his lifeblood, the sleeves of my shirt dripping red. His head bows. I place my palm on his forelock and rest my forehead on is nose. To think of everything we have lived through, everything we have survived. Desert storms, battles and worse. It's not right that he should end like this—end at the hands of a Star God minion.

Boots scuff the ground behind me; a small stone skips past. I don't bother looking up.

'Your horse is lost,' says the sheriff. 'Come now, and I promise you the gift of redemption.'

I roll back onto my heels. Cerberus's eyes are a dull red. 'Go to hell,' I say.

'As you wish.' The sheriff aims his reloaded blaster.

The weapon sparkles in the sunlight. The sheriff shines in his finely tailored clothes. A sharp contrast to myself, on the ground covered in dust and old blood.

I turn back to Cerberus, now all silver and frozen in place. It's almost over for him—for me.

But a light catches the corner of my eye. Green. I look up as it thunders over the roof of the saloon.

Hydraea.

Still free, she is clear to wreak havoc. Shifting and twisting in the midday heat, she aims one moment for the sheriff and the next for me. The

Original's blaster swings to the new threat, but the sheriff fails to lock onto Hydraea's roaming essence. My chimera swoops low then plunges into the side of my dying mech-horse.

'Take my power!' roars Hydraea as she melts into Cerberus's metal flank.

Suddenly, the stallion's eyes flare red, then green and then red again. The two chimera souls settle in the one mechanical and together they rise, rearing, sharp hooves clutching at the sky.

Panicking, the sheriff fires again. His Original blazes into the sky. But she misses her mark, clipping the side of the saloon. The people within scream as debris rains around them. They spill out into the road as half the building collapses.

The sheriff looks stunned, not nearly so certain of himself anymore. I call out encouragement as Cerberus and Hydraea work together to charge the Star God's creature down. His mech-blaster is torn from his hand. It tumbles to the ground. Then I glimpse flashes of silver, white and ivory. The sheriff's glamour falls. His magnificent, scaled wings burgeon into existence.

The Star God's minion keens out an inhuman cry. With a rush of air, he tries to flee. But my chimeras are swift. Cerberus's copper hooves fall, catching and tearing at the fragile wing membranes. The sheriff stumbles and tries to rise again. He labours, belling the tattered remnants of flesh hanging from his back to catch the air, and fails. His blood scatters, coating everything in a fine gold mist. Then he sinks to the ground beaten, his perfect form torn asunder by the wicked storm of my chimeras' collective ire.

The battle is done.

Another flash of green. Hydraea tears herself free of Cerberus's body. She circles a moment while I retrieve my blaster then returns to the metal of her own body. I try to thank her, but ill tempered to the end, she snarls at me, 'I help my friends.'

'I didn't know you were Cerberus's friend.'

'*Harrumph.*'

My heart soars as my stallion trots over to me. I pull myself up into the saddle. The blood from my shirt drips onto his mane and down his neck. It absorbs into the metal and with it comes a flash of renewed power in his eyes. It's not nearly enough to restore him to full health, but will do until I can find more blood. I re-holster Hydraea. She sighs with relief.

Then Cerberus is running. His hooves drum a steady beat on the sun-baked earth. The air carries the scents of dust and sun-scorched grass. The sheriff's blood on me tastes sickly sweet.

Cerberus heads for the desert. Home—the searing plains—the only place on this planet we can call home.

I take one last look back at the street and the broken saloon. The sheriff still sits in the middle of the road. Alive but damaged. His ruined wings are held aloft, stained bright with his golden blood. The townspeople surround him but his eyes are on me. He raises his bloodied hand, the sunlight illuminating their metallic colour. He holds his fingers open.

And I can't tell if he's bidding me farewell or cursing me.

Undertaker

The soldier's control tag feels feather-light against my palm. I thumb away the blood coating the small, flat, metal plate and check if its restrainer chip is still intact. It is. Good news for the Maderae, not so good for the next human forced to wear the technology.

I drop the tag into my burlap bag. The bloodied metal chimes wetly against the others nestled in the bottom. I sigh. It's a grim job, this collecting from the dead. But with tags in short supply due to a lack of the rare metal needed to manufacture them, it makes them valuable. They control humans, and control is the currency of the Maderae. It ensures their dominance over Earth. I should be thankful that the aliens need them, I suppose. Being a Collector makes me useful—it keeps me alive.

And it lets me keep searching for my sister, Dellar.

Mud sucks at my boots as I pick my way deeper into the battlefield. It's funny to think that once children played football here. Or perhaps not so funny. Now, it's no-man's land—the place between Upper Town and the River District, where warring factions of Maderae send their remote-controlled soldiers to defend Nest borders. In all my years, I've never actually seen the borders shift. Just watched the soldiers, who are sent to fight, keep dying.

The next corpse lies face up in the mud. A female. On seeing her my heart, as always, skips a beat. But then, as always, the body isn't my sister. Not Dellar.

I let out a breath. This woman's hair is different. The locks have been shorn in the fashion that all soldiers are shaved but the stubble still reveals the colour—blonde, not black. The thick copper collar at the woman's neck is another clue. It bears the blacksmith stamp of the Minor Nest, the sub-set of Maderae that control the Tag Industries building complex and public kitchens that make Upper Town. Not the ones who took my sister.

I push back the cowl of my long, black jacket, careful not to expose the wires of the weapons vest concealed beneath it. My artillery vest. Highly illegal but sure proof of protection. I'm useful to the Maderae now, working for them to retrieve lost tags, but everyone knows how quickly favour can turn to misfortune. It's better to be prepared.

My serrated knife slides easily out of my belt sheath. I glance at the woman's face, doubting I'll recognize her, but take the time to check anyway. It's why I call myself Undertaker. If I recognize any of the dead, I send word to the free rebel families. Not easy to do, but possible via the few humans that work in the public oil baths. That way the bodies can be taken home and given a decent burial. It's a small thing, but important—important to the parents whose children were harvested for soldiering.

Just like Dellar was.

But I don't know this woman. She is another sister or daughter dead with no family to mourn her.

I press the tip of my blade under the tag embedded in her temple. Levering it upwards, the plate pulls away with a slurping sound. Wires follow, thin elements that burrow back into the brain and link with the cortex. I slice through them and pull the tag away.

Wipe off the blood.

Put the tag in the bag.

It's the routine I follow, set by years of experience. And it's the humdrum of that routine that sees me taken unawares.

Ice-cold fingers wrap around my wrist.

A shocked breath hisses past my teeth. The knife slips from my hand and thuds to the ground. The dead woman; she is not dead. Her eyes, their green hue startling compared against her bloodied face, are open and pleading.

'Help me.' Her voice is thick, the words slurring on clotted blood.

'Holy hell! You're alive?'

The woman closes her eyes. She looks dead again, except for the fact that her chest is rising and falling.

How did I miss that?

A terrible mistake to make. I've just taken a tag from a living soldier.

I'm screwed if I'm caught.

I consider killing her. A knife wound amongst the other damage she already bears, won't be noticed. But even as the thought manifests, I know I can't do it. I'm no killer.

What to do?

I look around. The twins, Talison and Mordra, are mining the battlefield with me. Talison is dangerous, but Mordra is the larger concern. She's an Overseer. She discovers this, and I'm done. I like her, she's fair, but she'll have no choice but to tell the Maderae. For the moment though, her focus is still on her work.

It's not too late—if I could only bring myself to kill.

The woman at my feet moans again.

'Shhh,' I hiss. 'Quiet, or we'll both end up dead.'

The decision is made. I can't end her. Quickly, I dig into my bag and pull out a tag. I line it up with the hole in the woman's temple and press it back into place. Her blood works like glue, holding the metal tag in position. The restrainer chip won't work, obviously, but at least the woman will look the part of a controlled soldier. I reach under her arms and pull her upright. She's heavy, full of sinewy muscle. And she stinks like the battlefield—like rotten mud and old blood.

'Undertaker?'

I turn. Talison's whip crack voice echoes out across the field. A tangle of tags and wires hangs from his fist. 'Found one alive,' I say. 'Taking it back to the Minors.'

There's a moment's pause. His desire to claim my prize is clear. To return a live soldier gets you priority benefits for a day—your choice of food, an afternoon at the human brothel. It's tempting to let Talison take the woman. He's a Maderae sympathizer. Not that the aliens return his regard. The reward Talison would get in returning an untagged soldier to them would be no less than brutal.

But Mordra steps in. 'Let her be, Talison. The soldier will probably die before she gets it back to the barracks.'

Mordra is a sensible kind of woman. I respect that. 'Good chance of it,' I say. 'But I'll try. Can always dump her and take the tag if she dies.'

Talison sneers. But he does as his sister commands. He waits a moment longer, staring at me, and then turns. I watch long enough to see him kneel and pry a tag off another dead body.

***

The streets are deserted. I drag the soldier down their length. Her breath bubbles wetly by my ear, the bright red sound of a punctured lung. But, even so, the woman keeps pace. Her feet lift, fall and scrape their way along the ruptured bitumen. 'Don't take me back,' she whispers.

Her desperation resonates absolute. 'I'm not, soldier,' I say.

'Where to—?' Her voice fails her. She coughs and a spray of blood fans across her chin.

There's only one place to go. 'Sanctuary. I'm taking you home.'

'Home. Why?'

'Because I don't want to die today.'

The woman slumps against my shoulder. 'Dead is better than tagged.'

***

I pass by the Tag Industries complex with its ugly rectangular logo hung over the gated entry. Just ahead of it, the grease-slick sizzle sound of the public kitchens can be heard. Here the road is busier, full of people and Maderae. Oil, excrement, sweat—so many different smells. But the most overpowering is the blistering curry-coloured slop of crushed wheat, raw meat and chemicals that is the preferred nourishment for the Maderae. I turn us down a side street.

The place smells like a urinal. Piles of clustered rubbish, heaving with rats, loiter in the gutters. Ruined buildings, once the homes of free humans, line the footpaths. I ignore them. Sanctuary is not far; the hidden home to those few who still fight our alien invaders—just a few more metres…

But I don't make it.

Talison must have said something to Mordra. Something to convince her I needed investigating, something profound enough to have her call the Minor Clan Maderae down on me.

They round a corner in a flurry of black and silver—Talison, Mordra and three giant metal cockroach-like Maderae.

'Undertaker!' Mordra's voice echoes down the street.

I halt. The soldier-woman shuffles to a stop beside me. Her breathing is irregular, but she's not close enough to dying to save me from this predicament. I try to look innocent as I meet Mordra's gaze. 'Yes, Overseer. Is there a problem?'

'Hand over the soldier. The Minors will take it from here.'

I'd give anything to know what Talison has said to her. But wishing doesn't mean you get it. So I smile, but there is no warmth in it. 'If only I could.'

Mordra looks disappointed. For a moment her air of status falls away, and she becomes a woman with whom in a different time and place, I would have called a friend. 'I thought better of you, Undertaker.'

'Not me,' says Talison, all too keen to express his own opinion. 'Always pegged you more for an insurgent collaborator than a Collector.'

***

The Maderae know nothing of mercy. A mistake is never forgiven. The crime of human error is always dealt with swiftly, and in such a way they intend to deal with me.

The Maderaes' exoskeletons ripple like molten silver as they stride past the twins.

Crunch. Crunch. Crunch.

Their moulded metal legs piston up and down, the sharpened tips punching through the bitumen like butter. The Maderae are communicating. Their metallic sounding language, a chorus of clicks and whirs, bounces off the broken brickwork and rusted balustrades that line the street.

The soldier at my side stirs. It's as if the sound of her freedom being threatened inspires wakefulness. She struggles against me, trying to force herself upright. Her muscles bunch against my side, her breath catches. It seems the amount of effort expended to just push upright will be enough to end the woman. But then her weight is off me and she is standing on her own.

The Maderae stop. The mandibles of the first in the row begin to work. 'Submit for re-integration.' The alien has switched to speaking English, but the words sound painfully twisted around its metal voice cogs.

The soldier next to me sways on her feet. Her hand creeps to the small blade holstered at her side. It's an ineffectual weapon. 'I won't,' she whispers, her voice heavy with conviction. 'I can't.'

Her words recall to me all the soldiers I've seen before. The ones stored in the barracks with their dead eyes that stare at nothing and half clad bodies freezing in the winter air. Never once did I think they felt anything past the installation of their tags.

It would seem I was wrong.

And that my sister's fate is far worse than I imagined.

The three Maderae stride forward again, their maws opening and closing, silver mandibles chittering and clattering. I glance at the soldier. Her attention is fixed on the approaching enemy. Her knuckles are fitted tight to the handle of her blade. They gleam white like bone.

'Get behind me,' she says.

'I can protect myself,' I reply.

The air crawls cold against my skin as I peel back my jacket. Mordra's face blanches white as the wires and moulded copper plates of my artillery vest are revealed. My hidden weapon. The quartets of lasers built into the vest are strong enough to slice through anything—including Maderae.

The Maderae increase speed, their antennae sparking with the electricity that will knock me out if they get hold of me.

They come in fast, but time seems to slow. An instant turns to a minute. With time to spare I see everything. I see the soldier-woman dip into a crouch, useless blade held ready. I see the grey, filtered sunlight of the day glint off the Maderaes' carapaces. I see Talison's black cloak billow wide in a sudden gust of wind and Mordra desperately trying to pull him away—

Cool air rushes in through my nose and fills my lungs to full.

I reach across my chest.

My palm finds the engraved button positioned over my heart.

I press it.

Click.

Silence.

Nothing.

My breath hitches in my throat. It didn't work? Why didn't the vest work?

Time speeds up.

The soldier-woman is screaming at me, 'Run!'

And Mordra is screaming at her brother, 'Flee!'

But Talison's hatred of me runs too strong. He pulls away from his sister and follows in the Maderaes' footsteps. His face contorts, twisted with bloodlust. His jagged edged tag blade is out. 'Time to die, traitor.'

Mordra screams out again, 'Talison! NO!'

But he keeps on coming, just as the Maderae do.

Then I see my future.

As a soldier, rendered immobile, sitting on a cold hard bench.

As an unidentified body lying in the mud.

A corpse with a Collector's blade pressed against my temple.

'I can't let this happen.' I whisper to myself.

The soldier-woman turns at the sound of my voice. Her eyes are full of fire. She smiles a broken toothed smile. 'Better dead than tagged,' she agrees.

Her hand shifts to her side. I'd missed it before—missed the grenade hanging off her belt. The soldier-woman is still smiling as she pulls it free. The small click as she releases the pin sounds like thunder.

I don't have time to think of what's about to happen. The Maderae are on us. So close I can smell the oil in their joints, hear the hiss of their breaths.

The soldier-woman throws her missile. It lands, clattering between the legs of the closest Maderae. Mordra cries out one last time, a broken sound. Then she gathers herself and runs, leaving Talison to his fate. I'm glad she's safe. I like her, Talison's sister…

Sister.

Dellar.

I close my eyes and try to remember my own sister. But the details of her face elude me. Only a faint memory of her warm smile remains in this final moment. *She is waiting for me past this life*. At least, that is what I tell myself as I am thrown to the ground and surrounded by searing fire, heat and light.

***

Death is not at all like I expected. There is darkness and pain. In being dead, I would not have thought I would be aware of such things, or be possessed of the need to open my eyes.

But I am and so I submit. My vision is blurry at first, but then I make out falling dust, smell charred bitumen and taste blood in my mouth. My ears are ringing also, a high-pitched, distracting whine. There is a weight across me. The corpse of the soldier-woman. I push her off and sit up, choking on a lungful of air. The dead don't need to breathe. Of this fact I'm certain.

So I'm still alive it seems.

The soldier's body saved me.

I look around. A dark bundle of blood-soaked cloak is all that remains of Talison. And then there are the Maderae. Two lie useless, their bodies twisted hunks of metal. The third is down, but relatively intact.

Well, the exoskeleton is. The passenger it held was not so lucky. The life pod portion of the giant metal body has cracked open and from it, the translucent-skinned corpse of a Maderae Master half hangs out. Long clear tubes are pierced into the alien's back, curry-coloured liquid pulsing down their lengths. Its long, jelly-like fingers drape like tentacles over the polished metal exterior. Its eyes, eerily human, stare sightlessly into the distance. The creature is lifeless.

Disgusting yet inspiring. It's the first time I've seen a Maderae dead. I always assumed they couldn't be killed.

Interesting.

In the distance, the familiar sound of bitumen crunching beneath metal feet echoes out. More Maderae.

The seed of an idea suddenly blossoms in my mind. Do I dare do it? Is it even possible?

Better dead than tagged.

I launch across the broken road, past Talison and over the pieces of ruined Maderae armour. My fingers slip on the oily-feeling wrist of the creature within the exoskeleton. I shrug aside my revulsion, reach and pull again. This time the corpse with its two humanoid arms and legs slithers free, the tubes in its back wrenching away like plugs. I drop it to the ground, my lips pulled away from my teeth with distaste.

My palm is cleaned down the front of my cloak, a line of slime following it. I scramble up inside the exoskeleton. The seat in the pod is slippery and smells foul but no time to dwell on it. I survey the control console. Buttons and levers flash. Red, green and blue. *How do I close this thing?*

It takes a moment for me to notice the words written beneath the controls. Open Hatch. Close Hatch. Forward. Reverse. Front lasers.

English?

The controls are in English?

What the hell?

Then I see it.

The logo imprinted in the top corner of the metal console.

Ugly. Rectangular.

The logo that once belonged to the largest robotics company in the world.

Tag Industries.

Why would it be in an extraterrestrial machine?

Dots begin to join. Uncomfortable. Unclean. The connections I make are disturbing.

Connections I don't want to believe.

But wanting and seeing are two different things entirely. The truth shatters around me, hard and heavy like falling masonry.

It was all a lie.

We weren't invaded.

It was us.

Humans.

We subverted ourselves with our own technology.

My mind reels as the Maderae reinforcements round the corner. In the crunch of their steps and the hiss of their breaths, I hear, not for the first time today, the sound of my death approaching.

But the bravery of the soldier-woman has inspired me.

I press the Close Hatch button and reach for the laser controls. 'Better dead than tagged,' I whisper as I pull the triggers.

Bloodlines

I peel my fingers off the steering wheel. They ache, as does the finger where my red acrylic nail has snapped off. I must have hit my knuckles on the dash. My car is in the middle of the road, stationary but still idling. The deer lies dead on the verge, too far beyond help for me to bother getting out to look at it.

The sight of its twisted neck unsettles me. I look to the road that leads to Barrow. Just visible through the half-fogged windscreen, it snakes away into the distance, a snowy blur. Alaskan snow. Insidious. Incessant. Infinite. I straighten the steering wheel, check my rear-view mirror then ease my foot off the brake. The car rolls forward. I brake again.

Something else lies by the side of the road.

I brush at the condensation on the windscreen. The glass clears and the blurred form outside sharpens. A man. He is only noticeable by his bright red hair. It's almost luminous against the pristine snow. He lies beneath a leafless tree, his thin form clad in a dark green fleece jacket and blue pants. And he is curled in on himself, clenched into a ball with fists clutched tight to his chest. There is also more I wish I couldn't see. His lips, and how dark they are— his wrists with their motley patchwork of bruises and the blood on his face. I don't want to get out of the car. He's dead, I'm sure of it. And worse, it looks like he died in the same way my mother did and in the same way my brother, Charles, did.

And their loss is still too raw; an open wound in my heart.

Even so, I kill the engine and open the door. A blast of winter air rushes in, stealing my heat as it passes and leaving my lips tingling. I grab my jacket from the passenger's seat. The fabric is warm from the car's heater, but I'm still cold as I slip it over my shoulders.

I step out of the car. My shoes crunch through the snow and hit the frozen bitumen beneath. The injured man lies motionless. Knots form in my stomach; my throat is dry. I want to leave, but already know I won't.

Off the road and past the deer carcass, the going is difficult. My ankles buckle and roll as I cross the carpet of snow-covered rocks. Finally, I reach the tree. A sheen of frost coats the man's long hair, crusted blood lines his cheek and chin. It's as I thought—someone beat him and left him here to die.

Just like someone did to my mother.

Just like someone did to Charles.

I huddle deeper into my jacket. I should check the man for a pulse, but I don't want to touch him.

'Don't be such a coward, Nell,' I whisper.

***

An age ago, I came from the stars.
Came to rule this world.
But the humans, they fought back.
They stripped me of my body and bound my essence
to their bloodlines.
They used Winter's power to confine me.
But the magic in the blood of their descendants—
It has weakened with each generation.

***

The man's neck is pale like the snow. I lean in to press my fingers against the cold flesh, but hesitate. My hand hovers over his skin. My vision doubles and I tremble. I checked my brother's pulse the same way; leaned in, felt his dead flesh.

I hadn't dared to touch my mother's body.

Finally, I let my fingers drop to his throat. But instead of cold flesh, there is warmth and a faint pulse.

I step back, my skin crawling. My heel slips and I almost fall. I take another step back. The way he looks, the bruising, the blood—he should be dead. But the man's chest is rising and falling; his fingers are twitching.

He is alive.

Not like my mother.

Not like Charles.

I roll the man over and rip off my jacket. I lay it over his chest and curl my arms under his. His breathing hitches as I drag him, but he remains unconscious. It's hard going. He is heavy and the snow has fallen so deep and soft.

We get to the road. With a trembling hand, I open the rear door. The hinges screech with the cold. I half-lift, half-drag the man into the back seat. He flops down against the dark leather like a wet doll.

I slam the door shut and get into the front. I twist the key and the engine roars to life. The heater fires up to full, blasting warm air into the car's interior. I press the accelerator. Town is three kilometres away, at the bottom of the long, winding road.

***

Warmth.
It curls over skin.
Feather light and delicious.
With it, my bonds weaken again.
I savour the promise of resurrection.
Here I come. Here I come.

***

The car screeches to a halt in front of the Emergency entrance of the hospital. I jump out and rush through the doors, past the hospital security guards and into the waiting room. 'Help!' I scream. 'I need help.'

The receptionist looks startled for a moment and then bursts into action. Buttons are pressed; a phone is spoken into. Two nurses—one male, one female—appear with a stretcher from the doors leading from the examination areas. My heart sinks. I know one of them. She was my brother's best friend. Jess. She lives at the end of my street with her strange grandmother, the one who always stares at me like I'm a freak.

Jess catches my eye. She pauses. The look on her face is the same one her grandmother gives me. *Freak.* But then she moves again. I lead them out the exit.

Jess doesn't look happy when she sees what is on the back seat. 'Jesus, Nell,' she whispers. 'What the hell happened to him?'

'I don't know. I found him in the snow.'

Jess looks at me, her dark eyes sharp. 'Just like Charles?'

I shift uncomfortably. 'Yes. Just like Charles.'

Jess stares at me for a moment longer. She shakes her head. 'Let's get him inside.'

I choose to wait for news about the man. I could go home, but it doesn't feel right leaving him here alone. It's warm in the waiting room and for the moment, I'm happy to be away from the cold. All that snow. I always feel so smothered by it.

I pull my knees up to my chin, close my eyes, and rest them against my crossed wrists. I feel drowsy. All the warmth. It makes me want to sleep.

I press my eyes against the back of my wrists. The darkness behind my eyelids seems to swirl. It's hypnotizing. I slip further into myself—and suddenly I am dreaming.

I am standing in the snow beneath a tree. The red-headed man lies at my feet, his body curled in to protect itself and his fists clenched to his chest. His face begins to blur. It changes to become my mother's—all bloodied. Then my brother's—all broken. Curious, I lean in to look closer. The man's features keep shifting, cycling like terrible photographs. The red-headed man. Mum. Charles. Then the face solidifies and I am looking at my brother. His eyes are open. 'Stay in the cold, Nell,' he says to me. 'It's coming.'

***

I wake with a start. Disorientated, it takes a moment for me to realize I am still in the hospital. The receptionist continues to sit behind the desk. A loose line of people wavers past me, waiting their turn for service. I glance across the tops of the green tartan waiting chairs and over to the examination area doors.

Jess is standing there with a police officer. I don't recognize the woman. She must be one of the new recruits recently arrived from Anchorage. Her uniform is crisp and new. She looks young. Jess hands something to her. I see a brief flash of scarlet before the tiny object disappears into the woman's palm. Then Jess speaks. The words are too faint for me to hear. When she finishes, the police officer glances over at me.

The woman nods to Jess then heads towards me, wading her way past the people and through the chairs. 'Ms. Smith?'

'Yes.'

'I'm Constable Withers. You brought in the injured man?'

I am suddenly feeling very hot. Have they turned the heat up in here? 'Yes.'

'Would you mind telling me where you were going when you found him?'

'I was coming back from my work Christmas party.'

The woman pauses. 'Christmas party?'

The heat prickles up my neck. My vision doubles. 'Is there a problem with that?'

'Yes,' replies the police woman. 'It's February. Christmas is long gone.'

Inexplicable fury boils my blood. I grit my teeth. My fingers curl.

'Ms Smith?' she asks, tilting her head.

My fist connects with her chin, a solid whack. Her head snaps to the side and she stumbles backwards. I follow, to hit her again, but fall as I'm tackled to the ground by a security guard. I lie, winded, bruised and burning inside. I'm rolled over to my stomach. Handcuffs clamp down on my wrists. My nose and cheek are pressed into cold vinyl flooring that smells like antiseptic. I roar, my voice sounding more animal than human.

***

Imprisoned as I am, I can only guess at the passage of time.
I am certain to make mistakes.
But no matter.
The heat has worked its power and the blood bonds are loosened.
I have already begun to claw free, to crack the veneer.
Not long now.

***

The interview room is small and smells like stale coffee and cigarettes. I'm calm now but confused. Is it really February? The funeral for Mum and Charles was in late November. A cold and wet day. Grey. Bleak. Then on December 24th, I remember feeling depressed but deciding to show my face at the work Christmas party anyhow. After that, nothing. What happened to the last couple of months?

The heater on the wall is forcing in super-heated air. It's too hot in here. I am suffocating. A bead of sweat trickles down my spine. I look up at Constable Withers sitting across from me. Her left cheek and eye are swollen. She doesn't look impressed.

'I'm sorry I hit you,' I say, trying my best to sound as sincere as I feel. 'I'll understand if you press charges.'

But she isn't interested in talking about the punch. The woman very carefully reaches over and places a clear plastic bag on the table. I lean in to look. Inside is the shattered end of a long, red, acrylic fingernail.

'Do you recognize this?' she asks.

'No,' I say.

'Can I see your hands?'

I look down at the fingers curled in my lap, at the bruised knuckles and the broken, still throbbing, stub of my scarlet red, acrylic nail. I look back at the woman. 'I…ah… I guess it could be mine.'

'It could be,' says the constable. 'Would you like to guess where we found it?'

I wipe the back of my hand across my forehead. 'In my car?'

'No, Ms Smith.'

'Where then?'

The policewoman pushes the nail closer to me. 'This was lodged in the cheek of the man you took to hospital. Deep. Could have only been put there with force.'

My stomach churns. The heater—it's making me dizzy. I look at the jagged nail sitting on the table. Charles, Mum, the red-headed hitchhiker.

Did I hurt those people?

And then I feel sick. I know I did.

But why would I do that?

Then a voice, thick and heavy, interrupts my thoughts—invades my mind. *'Because you are the vessel, and heat is the key to your lock. When I am free, you are trapped by my will.'*

I take in a shuddering breath. My mind shifts, and I suddenly recall the sensation. This has happened to me before—this shifting—three other times and in the presence of three victims.

Mum. Charles. The red-headed hitchhiker.

I try to scream. Control of my body is torn from me. My awareness is shunted aside as another rises to claim my place. There is pain. I am set adrift. The threads of my identity are left to waver aloft. I watch, helpless, through eyes now not my own. The alien force stretches my arms wide and bares my teeth. Then it roars, an inhuman sound torn from my human throat.

Withers pulls her gun. The being within me throws my body across the desk.

I am powerless to stop as Withers's throat is seized in my fist. Her eyes bulge as my long nails tear into her tender flesh and rip her windpipe open. The creature in my body leans in to savour the look on her face. But I see her features blur. They cycle…my mother, my brother. And I want to scream with grief.

Then I hear Charles's voice in my mind. 'You're possessed, Nell.'

I sob silently, unable to use my voice for myself.

Charles had spoken to me the day he died. His voice was urgent as he stood in the snow outside our house. 'I don't know why you don't remember, Nell.' He'd wiped his hand across a face worn thin with grief. 'Jesus. You—your essence—just *disappeared*. You became some kind of animal. I haven't told anyone else yet. But you did it—' He choked back his emotion. 'You killed Mum.'

'You're talking crazy, Charles,' I remember saying as I'd huddled down, scared, into the warmth of my jacket. 'How dare you blame me? Mum's dead. I don't know who did it, and I'm just as upset about it as you.'

Charles's face had tightened. 'Nell. Come with me. I've spoken to Jess's grandmother. She used to be a psychiatrist. She can help us.'

'I don't think so…'

There is a crash. The door to the interview room smashes open. The creature swings our gaze up. Jess stands in the doorway, led by another officer. Withers's blood coats the walls, and the sudden smell of the policeman's fear floods the room. But not Jess. She looks shocked, but isn't afraid. She takes in the details of the scene, the still body of Withers. Her eyes narrow. 'I won't give up on you, Nell,' she says calmly, 'because Charles was my friend and he loved you.'

The alien curls my lip into a wry grin. 'Your grandmother's blood flows in you. Old World blood—ancient, resilient.' It laughs aloud. 'But it's not strong enough to stop me.' My body is forced to walk towards Jess. My arm extends and the creature, viper fast, snatches at her neck.

Jess is brave. I rage, impotent, behind the dominating presence of the creature, unable to help her. I watch the emotions play across Jess's face. Her mouth is bared in a grimace; her dark eyes blaze. But there is no fear. She faces down the animal inside me, even as it crushes her neck.

I take strength from her strength.

I slam my awareness against the creature's mind, to no avail. It ignores me and uses the length of my own nails to pierce Jess's skin. I growl, frustrated as her blood coats my hand. Jess is turning blue. I am about to start hitting out again, but then the grimace on her mouth changes.

She's smiling.

The alien hesitates. I stop too. We both feel the sting in the blood on my hand. The tingle turns into a burn. My body lurches. I can't control its movement any more than my captor can. Jess is thrown, still conscious, to the floor.

The presence inside me wails. It tries to tear at the inner lining of my skin, but its hold on me is weakening. Jess's blood. It's burrowing into me and driving the creature out. With its grip slipping, I use all the strength of mind I possess to *push*. It lets go. Control of my body returns. The alien's essence is forced up my throat. I gag then vomit. A puddle of green-black fluid sprays out across the floor.

I am alone in my body.

On my knees, I look for Jess. She is half lying, half sitting on the floor across from me. Between us hovers a dark cloud of smoke, humanoid in shape and with eyes bright like the inside of a furnace.

Jess does nothing. Can't she see it? Her eyes look past it—through it—and are firmly fixed on me.

The creature moans, an unearthly sound, as its vaporous form is sucked into the wound on Jess's neck. Jess's skin ripples for a moment and then I hear a final howl, a long drawn out note of anguish.

Then silence.

Jess heaves in breaths of air. Every now and then, I see her face ripple as the creature within her tries to break free. But Jess's eyes are *almost* her own as she lifts them. 'It's alright, Nell,' she says. 'My grandmother will do as Charles asked. She'll help you get better.'

I start to cry. Jess reaches over and grasps my hand. 'It's okay. You're sick. You can't help what happened.'

But maybe I could have—maybe I could have fought harder to save Mum and Charles. Maybe I tried to but failed.

I can't remember.

My guilt, a stony weight, threatens to drown me. I barely notice the other people filing into the room. I don't hear their shouts of anger or their gasps of horror at what has happened. I simply bow my head and let them restrain me. The handcuffs they use feel cold against my skin.

Wolverslinger

Three days ago he was shot dead in the street. Marshal Matthew Payton, my husband. He was still lying in the dust, blood leaking from the side of his mouth, when I chose to pick up his fallen guns. And the hired mercenary that murdered my husband? Well I killed him right back. A bullet. Dead between the eyes. He didn't look none too impressed at being killed by a woman, but there you have it. A man's destiny is never truly his own.

But now I am left with questions.

Who hired him?

Who wanted my husband dead?

Frustrated, I slam my hand against my desk. The jail cell keys hanging on the rack at the end jangle. My thinking has it pinned on Old Man Cassidy. There isn't any proof, but it's got to be him. Marshal before Matthew, Cassidy was out voted in the last election. The old man didn't take the forced retirement too well. He was thrown out of the saloon later that day, drunk as a skunk and hollering that the townsfolk would regret it if we didn't give him his job back. 'You ungrateful bastards don't deserve no protectin',' he'd yelled as Matthew had bundled him off to the cells.

There's a rap at the door. Sharp. I can hear dust and grit in the sound of it—a traveller's hand rapping. It's late. I've half a mind to ignore it. But then I recall. The townsfolk voted and made me Marshal, meaning their problems are my problems. 'C'mon in,' I answer.

The door creaks open. It's dark out. No stars. But the lantern hanging from the corner of the 'Marshal's Office' sign outside reveals the outline of a man. His features are in shadow, but the light exposes his hand as it pushes the weathered door. A slinger's hand—rough and scarred by a fast life, hard lived. The man's boots, worn just as rough, scuff the threshold as he enters. The hilt of a silver knife hanging holstered at his belt catches the lamplight as he moves.

I don't trust slingers. Especially ones armed with knives. I keep my voice professional but cold. 'What can I be helpin' ya with this evenin'?'

A pause. Long enough for the cool evening air to carry the scent of the man to me—horse and oiled leather. 'A iced down whiskey would do me just perfect, Marshal.'

I smile, recognizing the deep, smoky voice. It's Clay, my brother. I get up from my desk, pushing aside the front page of the Prairie Times with its picture of Matthew lying dead in the street. 'Clay!' I say, glad to see him.

Clay looks pale as he steps into the lamplight. Paler than even last time I saw him. Even his fiery red hair seems to have lost its sheen. He's haunted looking, like he's seen bad things—things that don't sit too well with the soul. But it's no different to how he's looked for the past year. Ever since Cassidy lost his job and hired Clay to help out at his ranch. Bloody Cassidy. If only I could convince my brother to stop working for him. But Clay's already told me in the past he won't be quitting any time soon.

I step in to hug my brother. His chest feels metal-hard against mine. 'It's right good to see ya,' I say.

Clay pulls away. His dark eyes search my face. He sure looks a hell of a lot older than he is. 'I heard 'bout Matthew,' he says. 'I'm real sorry I couldn' make his funeral.'

I clench my jaw. I'd had to stand in the midday heat alone to watch the gravedigger fill in Matthew's grave. Knowing that Clay was away on business, too far away to arrive in time, hadn't made me any less sour. Somehow I'd hoped my big brother would find a way to be there. I shrug. 'Ya had your reasons.'

Clay's broad hand engulfs my shoulder. His skin feels hot, almost burning, through the fabric of my shirt. 'I know I'm late, but I'm here now. What can I do to help?'

The heat of my brother's touch concerns me, but I know better than to mention it. I try to keep my voice light. 'Not much ya can do,' I say, 'Unless ya can make the dead killer talk.'

Clay smiles a smile that doesn't reach his eyes. 'I'm a man of many talents,' he says. 'Show me the body.'

***

The corpse of Matthew's murderer is in the cool room behind the saloon. Without an established identity, it lies waiting for the state sheriff's deputies to arrive and take possession of it. The fabric it's wrapped in, an old red and white checked tablecloth, is stained with blood at one end.

I hold the lantern high. Clay leans in to sniff the body. 'Three days dead,' he mutters as if to himself. He pulls his knife free and cuts the tablecloth away.

I expect to see the corpse I wrapped up in the street. A body with a blown-in skull. But I don't.

Instead, the body is whole—fully formed as if it's only sleeping. There's no sign of a bullet hole anywhere. 'I shot 'im in the head,' I say, confused. 'What the hell is goin' on?'

Clay positions his knife over the heart of the corpse. He glances up. 'This ain't no normal man, sis. It's a wolver. You need to be piercin' them both in the head and the heart to kill 'em properly. And this one'll be wakin' up soon if I don't make sure it stays dead. Ya best wait outside.'

'What's a goddamn wolver?'

Clay's knife hovers like a viper waiting to strike. His eyes glint red in the dim lamplight. 'Nothin' you want to be meetin',' he says.

I shudder. Something about his tone has me holding my tongue.

I leave the cool room door ajar and wait behind it. There's silence for a full three seconds. Then Clay mutters, 'This is for Matthew.'

A wet thud—the sound of Clay's knife plunging into dead flesh.

A pause.

A deep-throated scream.

Scrabbling and the thump of a fist connecting with flesh.

A spray of blood shoots out past the edge of the door and across the ground. Done waiting, I unholster my gun and wrench the door open.

The cool room is no longer clean. On a floor slick with blood, two figures grapple. My brother and the corpse now animated. The mercenary throws my brother over his shoulder. A glint of silver catches my eye—Clay's knife sticking out of the dead man's chest.

The dead mercenary seems oblivious to the weapon. It remains lodged, moving with him as he rolls his shoulders and stalks towards Clay. The edges of the man's shape blur and shift as he walks. One step, his shoulders thicken. The next, his face tapers and elongates into a dog-like snout. Teeth lengthen. Hair sprouts across his chest and tracks up the line of his neck.

No longer a man.

A wolver?

Clay was right. The bloody thing is damn well terrifying.

The creature slews sideways, claws raking in to slice at my brother. Clay slips backwards, moving faster than I've ever seen him move before—faster than I've seen any man move before. Then he pivots and leaps, his arms clamping around the wolver's chest. Face to face with the creature, Clay squeezes. Corded muscles bulge beneath his sleeves. The beast lifts his chin and howls, an animal sound. Clay snarls in response.

And as he does, I see more changes, but this time in my brother—his eyes, no longer brown, are white like a dead man's. His chest where it's pressed against the wolver is glowing red. I swallow my horror.

The creature head-butts Clay. My brother's grip slips and the light emanating from his chest fades. The wolver's arms slither free. He grasps Clay around the waist and flings him against the far wall. The cool room rocks with the force of the blow. Clay grimaces. As he leans over to clutch at his chest, I notice the front of his shirt is charred.

My heart hammers. My gun rests cold in my hand. I should shoot. Why am I not shooting?

The wolver lifts Clay by the neck. It presses him up against the wall and tightens its grip, long claws drawing blood. Clay's boots scrabble and slip against the slick floor. His breaths rattle—ragged gurgles around the crushing pressure of the wolver's grip.

My gun is up and the trigger pulled in one swift movement. The weapon booms, filling the air with the stink of gunpowder. The bullet hits true, and the beast staggers but doesn't fall. He's stronger, it seems, than he was three days ago in his guise as a man.

The wolver's gaze turns to fix on me. It looks pissed. In its gold eyes hangs the promise of my death. My brother reads the same. 'NO!' he screams.

Clay is thrown again. This time he hits the rear wall of the cool room with a solid thud. Again the room rocks. The wolver turns, coming for me. Its long toe claws clicking on the metal floor. I fall back a step, my gun cocked. Sweat runs down the length of my spine. My breathing sounds too loud in my ears.

The creature growls, his long teeth show as white points of sharpened bone against his black lips. I shuffle back another step.

This is it.

I'm a dead woman.

I shoot again. The bullet ricochets off the wolver's forehead. He takes another step. Another shot. The bullet flies wide.

The wolver's fingers are like vices as they close around my neck. Their clawed tips rake my skin. I clench my teeth and press the barrel of my gun to his chin. I fire. Round after round. Two, three and four. The gun clicks empty. The monster still stands.

Still stands.

Until.

A hand reaches over the wolver's shoulder. My brother's. I'd know his slinger fingers anywhere. They close around the knife still embedded in the chest of the monster. Clay pulls it free, releasing a torrent of blood.

And plunges the blade into the wolver's skull.

The creature's eyes bulge as the bone splits and separates. It slumps to the ground, finally dead. I land on my knees. The animal's blood, hot and acid coats my face. I gag on the taste of it—metal and ash mixed with wet pepper. It's in my mouth, in my throat. I can't seem to catch my breath. I cough and slump sideways to the floor.

Clay carries me outside and lays me down on the good, clean dirt. He leans over me, his eyes now black instead of white. My blood is burning. My heart races. Clay's hand grasps mine. 'Merry,' he says. 'Ya've bin infected with the wolver virus. It's in their blood. Shit. I can't stop it and I ain't allowed to let ya turn, baby sister.' The muscles bunch in his cheeks. 'I gotta protect the townsfolk—gotta kill any blasted wolver I find. There can't be no exceptions.'

I have questions. But my throat is burning and I can't say the words.

'We got two choices,' says Clay, 'but we gotta decide quickly.' The lines around his mouth deepen. 'What do I do, sis? Kill or change ya?'

I don't want to die.

Clay seems to understand. 'I can make ya like me. Not…not exactly human anymore but useful.' My brother leans in even closer. 'I won't be lying to ya, it's not an easy life, Merry. But Cassidy—he'll help ya learn to live with it, just like he helped me.'

Cassidy?

Clay opens the ruined front of his shirt. Beneath the fabric, a flat, copper metal plate sits fixed to the skin over his heart. Heat radiates off it, warm against my cheek. 'A wolver attacked me last year. Cassidy found me on the prairie. He fitted this tech to me to save my life. He made me like him. A Wolverslinger.'

Wolverslinger?

'He ain't from Earth, Merry. Not human like us. But he's on our side. He taught me 'bout the wolvers, 'bout how they aren't from Earth either. He taught me to hunt them. Together we' been keepin' the town safe.'

Matthew?

Again my brother seems to read my mind. He tips his chin towards the creature's corpse. 'Matthew died 'cause that one wanted revenge for me killin' its mate last month. Somehow it found out ya both were family. I'm real sorry. I didn' get here in time to do my job.'

The heat in my blood escalates. Hot and acid. Desperate for the pain to stop, I find my voice. The words come out sounding more like a growl, 'Change me.'

Clay nods. The lines around his mouth deepen. His silver knife is back in his hand. 'Only way to do it is cut out ya heart. But don't worry, baby sis. It's not the end. Cassidy will fix it.' He taps the metal plate on his chest. 'He'll give you a new one.'

A new heart.

A new life.

A chance to honour Matthew's memory.

I tighten my grip on the gun still in my hand. 'Do it,' I whisper.

Acknowledgements

I would like to thank the various editors who have worked with me on the stories in this collection and the exceptional beta readers who have given their valuable feedback.

Special mentions go to the following people. Judy Tait and Kat Pekin for their continued friendship, their shared love of words, wine and cheese and the valuable feedback they give. To Margaret McGraw, Misty Massey and Emily Lavin Leverett, the outstanding Falstaff Books editors who worked with me on my story *Cards and Steel Hearts* and helped earn me my first ever Aurealis Award nomination. To Aiki Flinthart, for reaching out and offering both her friendship and generous, in-depth commentary on my stories—thank you! And to my mother, Maria, who courageously battles the first draft reads and kindly tears them apart with her keen eye.

And as always, my sincerest thanks goes to my family. To Darren, Piper and Dakota. I write about strange worlds, but you are the world to me.

References

'Saloons and Stardust' first appeared in *Helios Quarterly Magazine – Vol2. Issue 1 Commercial Cosmonauts & Hired Guns*, Radiant Crown Publishing, March 2017.

'Cards and Steel Hearts' first appeared in the anthology *Lawless Lands: Tales from the Weird Frontier*, Falstaff Books, June 2017.

'Gunfire, Gas and Ruin' first appeared in *Andromeda Spaceways Magazine #72*, Andromeda Spaceways, September 2018.

'In Salt and by Starlight' first appeared in *AntipodeanSF* magazine, Issue 250, May 2019.

About the Author

Pamela Jeffs is a speculative-fiction author living in Queensland, Australia with her husband and two daughters. Her work has been published previously in various magazines and anthologies and has been twice nominated for Australian Aurealis Awards.

Prior to pursuing her passion for writing, Pamela's background was in interior and exhibition design. This allowed her to collaborate with a multitude of talented artists and designers across a number of artistic platforms.

Saloons and Stardust is her second collection, and features both new and previously published work.

To discover more books by Pamela Jeffs and be notified of new releases, deals and specials, visit and subscribe at:

www.pamelajeffs.com
Twitter: @Pamela_Jeffs
Facebook: @pamelajeffsauthor

Discover other titles by Pamela Jeffs at:
www.pamelajeffs.com

Including:

Red Hour and Other Strange Tales